Thomas Narcisse Doutney

I Told You So

Or, an autobiography

Thomas Narcisse Doutney

I Told You So
Or, an autobiography

ISBN/EAN: 9783337013356

Printed in Europe, USA, Canada, Australia, Japan

Cover: Foto ©Raphael Reischuk / pixelio.de

More available books at **www.hansebooks.com**

I TOLD YOU SO;

OR,

An Autobiography.

BEING

PASSAGES FROM A LIFE NOW PROGRESS-
ING IN THE CITY OF BOSTON,

AN INTEREST IN WHICH IS NOT EXCITED SIMPLY
BECAUSE FOUNDED ON FACT, BUT THAT
THE INCIDENTS THEREIN RELATED
ARE THEMSELVES THE FACTS.

BY

Mrs. T. NARCISSE DOUTNEY.

"And though calamities have crossed thee;
And misery been heaped on thy head."

Illustrated.

SOLD BY SUBSCRIPTION ONLY,
1873.

To

THE FRIENDS;

WHO, IN THE SPIRIT OF HUMANITY AND KINDNESS,

EXTENDED TO ME IN MY DARKEST HOUR

MATERIAL AID;

AND WHAT IS FAR MORE DELICATE AND RARE,

HEARTFELT SYMPATHY;

AND

TO THE PUBLIC;

WITH THE HOPE THAT THIS FEARFUL EXPOSÉ OF DISSIPATION,

AS PORTRAYED IN THE PHASE OF DRINK, MAY ADD ITS MITE TOWARDS THE

ERECTION OF A BARRIER MIGHTY TO STAY THE TIDE OF

INTEMPERANCE

ROLLING OVER THE LAND ; AND DESTROYING IN ITS

RESISTLESS COURSE THE FAIREST BULWARK,

OUR YOUNG MEN,

This Book,

WITH THE COMPLIMENTS OF THE AUTHOR,

IS RESPECTFULLY DEDICATED.

CONTENTS.

INTRODUCTION.

THE first time I heard Anna Dickinson speak, she stated that she had known poverty.

The time had been she was not able to buy a pair of gloves worth one shilling; that she had worked hard, and yet was poor.

She had decided it would be more profitable to give a poor lecture than receive poor pay.

I indorse her decision; and write a poor book, because of the very same reason, — poor pay.

Byron, by force of inspiration, wrote his " Bride of Abydos " in one night.

I, by force of poverty, write my book in one week.

He wrote for fame !

I write to pay my board.

His motive was the more elevated !

Mine, the more urgent.

Yes, — I am poor; worse still, — I am in debt. I owe —

"The butcher, the baker,
The candlestick maker," —

and see no way of canceling my indebtedness.

Everything I own in the world is at the pawnbroker's, — my watch, my brooch, my wedding-ring; and I see no way of redeeming them.

The spot on earth most sacred has passed into the hands of strangers.

Others walk the halls, enjoy the grounds, bury their dead; where my feet once trod, my eyes once feasted, my dead once reposed.

Reduced thus from affluence to poverty; alone, dwelling upon these things; 'I determine in some way to recover the lost.

Behold the reason why I write a book!

That it will be sensational, is not my fault; my life has been one long sensation.

That, "*à la Trollope,*" it will have its white and its black marks, is not my fault; some people *are* white, others black.

Unknown to friend or foe, I launch this manuscript upon the sea of literature; alike indifferent, whether the frail bark outrides the storm, or founders in sight, so that the purchase money, borne by the retreating wave, be washed to my feet.

BOSTON, 1873.

AN AUTOBIOGRAPHY.

CHAPTER I.

I AM BORN.

"Queen of the sisters twelve, Imperial June!"

"And a babe was cradled in her bosom."

ALL hail! beautiful June! month of roses; and of skies, whose blue arch, bending, lovingly embraces the fragrant earth, as bridegroom his beloved bride.

Beautiful June! in whose long, delicious days, summer arrives at the perfection of her charms; whose gentle airs, enameled fields, running streams; revive the invalid, delight the child, while the hours of Nature's lover.

Upon the sixteenth day of thy month, O beautiful June! I was born!

About four miles from the seaport of B—— is the large, agricultural town of W——.

Its inhabitants are mostly tillers of the ground. Still, the quiet beauty of the place, together with its reputed healthfulness, induced a few men of means and education to locate themselves there, and engage in amateur farming.

Earliest among these, of Puritan stock, both military and civic honors making his own name distinguished, came my maternal grandfather, Judge H——.

Although a gentleman, and companion of the learned, he soon ingratiated himself with his more lowly neighbors; securing at the same time, their respect and sincere regard. So well, too, and profitably, he managed his lands, that by degrees his opinion became their law.

Away from the main road, upon rising ground, stood the old-fashioned family mansion; completely embosomed in roses, the place was familiarly known as " Rose Hill."

Three daughters graced this pleasant home. The youngest, the fairest, met; and — true to her romantic nature — loved a wild but generous-hearted seaman. Against the judgment of her father, she persisted in marrying the youthful Captain.

If ever there was a love match, they made one.

Though separation, incident to his profession, and sorrow, were mingled in their cup ; neither — to the hour when the waters closed over the form of the idolized husband — had cause to regret their union.

I was their first child.

The preparation that heralded my advent, I have been told, was wonderful. Such embroidery ! such laces ! such trimming ! such tucking ! and all the Liliputian *trousseau,* the work of loving fingers and a loving heart; indulging, as each small garment was shaped, hopes and anticipations, as only the prospect of a first babe can inspire.

At length the long-expected time arrived.

After hours of agony, which almost cost the young mother her life; at the close of a quiet Sabbath, just as the sun's last rays glorified tree and flower, welcomed with smiles and prayers, upon the sixteenth day of thy month, O beautiful June! I **was born!**

CHAPTER II.

I AM A BABY.

"A babe in a house is a well-spring of pleasure."

Most infants are lovely only in mother's and nurse's eyes. But it has come down, that — skipping over the flabby, lobster period — I presented to admiring friends the grateful spectacle of a rosy, live baby; who, with large, wondering eyes, looked the world — into which it had such difficulty entering — full in the face.

Could I have foreseen what she would have given in answer to that appealing look, I would resolutely, then and there, have shut mine eyes upon her forever.

That was not to be.

I was to see life; and through the seeing, find my happiness, and — my misery.

A chance neighbor, studying my youthful orbs, impressed with the idea that I should probably find a use for them, meaningly remarked: "Well! she's got eyes, ain't she?"

My father, swelling with pride, assented; adding, "The child seems six months old!"

A disputed mark upon my tiny fore-finger, was settled by my mother declaring it to be strawberries; and the subject still further clinched by my devouring, of that delicious fruit, nearly a cupful when three days old.

This feat, together with my observant eyes, secured an infantile fame; and many was the gossip who came to look at the cup, and gaze upon me.

Of one heaven-given right I was deprived.

I never lay in maternal arms drawing sustenance from its natural source, my mother's fair breast.

The suffering incident to giving me birth was too intense, and too prolonged, to allow of one other effort in my behalf.

Nature avenged herself!

I was the victim!

Still, I throve. To compensate, A BOTTLE, emblem of my lost happiness, was placed in my puny grasp; and immediately became my constant companion.

Looking back, I am free to say, that, could I have anticipated, I should have adopted it on the spot as my future COAT OF ARMS.

I think it would have been pleasant ·to have enjoyed evermore this purely physical state of existence; holding on to the "em-blem" until full, then sinking off into the sleep of the innocent.

But Fate had other — any better? — things in store for me; and Time, leagued with Fate, ignoring my private wishes, car ried me out of babyhood into childhood.

2

CHAPTER III.

I AM A CHILD.

" For a child is in a new world, and learneth somewhat every moment."

I AM afraid Fear was a little too indiscriminately mingled with the motive power of my earlier years, to have allowed their being perfectly happy.

I learned to walk through the base motive!

I took my first step in mortal fear!

At the house of a friend, answering some summons, a darkey thrust his sooty visage inside the door.

Now I am speaking of ante-Lincoln days; when, as yet, our colored brothers had not come up to our houses, our tables, our very bed-chambers, so to speak ; and the moment that vision of darkness met my childish eye, although I had literally never taken one step in my future career, I rose from the cricket whereon I had been planted, and made straight for the sheltering arms of my mother; putting, in unquestioning faith, her love between me and, as I thought — the devil!

I had now found my feet.

Being of the " female persuasion," I did not have to hunt for my tongue. My friends will testify to that.

I was about to moralize — but hark! an agonizing scream falls on my ear. Once heard, above all, once *uttered*, never forgotten.

Yes — her hour has come ! The woman next room, — childbirth pangs upon her, — obedient to the fiat " In sorrow shalt thou bring forth," pays the penalty of her sex and suffers more than words can tell!

Everywhere; these same shrieks, constantly ascending to the ear of the Father
never closed to the cry of his children
must, one would think, shut out the very
music of heaven.   •

The silence of death has succeeded.

Is it that?

Happily, to the babe.

I have a bachelor cousin (what does *he*
know about it?) who says, " Better if all
thus died."

I agree!

Population might not get on so fast, but
it would be a good thing for the little
ones!

Once here, however, and likely to remain,
who can understand them? even our own?

We bring them into the world; feed
them; clothe them; are always with them;
yet in too many instances know them, as
we do the moon, by *outside* observation.

With the surface part of my being kindly cared for, I grew on; not much pains being taken to sound the depths, comprehend and train the hidden nature, which was my true self.

To feed and to clothe, is that all?

In modern days, chances are against the child through this undue attention to the external.

I do not complain; but I say, if more thought had been given to the best development of a highly sensitive organization; more labor bestowed upon the heart, less upon the head; I, for one, should have come up a better woman.

Clearly, I combined the elements of two distinct lives.

The one, bright and joyous; mischief and prank filling the house with sunshine. The other, dreamy and sad; influenced by emotions difficult to explain, but *with* which my playmates had no sympathy.

Never mind. I was full of vitality, and thoroughly enjoyed everything going, excepting — dolls.

Being a girl, I know I ought, but somehow I didn't.

Imagination was not at fault. Mine, however, would not take that direction.

I had no pleasure in tugging round the senseless things; making believe keep house; and all the rest of the tiresome programme.

I loved flowers. Already delighted in books. Adored music. A pity! as temperaments peculiarly susceptible to sweet sounds, are equally so to sorrow.

None *had*, thus far, come to me. None *might*.

Beloved by parents, petted by friends, I unconsciously slipped from happy childhood into sweet, mysterious girlhood.

CHAPTER IV.

MY GIRLHOOD.

" Beauty, is modesty and grace in fair retiring girlhood."

"Induce not precocity of intellect, for so shouldst thou nourish vanity."

THE other day I saw a picture, very beautiful in its whole conception.

Two figures, mother and daughter, are upon an eminence.

Wearily, the mother is looking backward; over the long, winding path her feet have trodden to reach this spot.

Eagerly, the daughter is looking forward into the dim distance; trying to locate the way her feet shall take.

I place myself beside the mother.

My past returns.

Its memories of youthful aspirations, so

crushed; youthful plans, so blighted; youth
ful friendships, so dead; that I only feel
sorrow in contemplating this ardent, high-
spirited maiden, knowing the certain disappointment to which she goes.

Only the phlegmatic really enjoy!

Once I met a person who boldly asserted
the same; and who, if launched again upon
life, would beg to leave behind — her heart!

I was no longer alone.

A fair-haired, blue-eyed girl, rivaled me
in my mother's love. I do not wonder. So
sweet-tempered, so thoughtful was the dear
child; a willing help in all the various domestic cares, which, to my shame, I invariably shirked.

But I do not think my father ever gave to
his second, the blind affection he lavished
upon his wayward first-born.

" Whom the gods love die young."

Endeared to all within her sweet influence, scarcely had fifteen brief summers passed, than, leaving us forever to mourn her loss, my sister died !

And one other; to his latest hour, will bear in his " heart of hearts " the memory of a dearly loved, and early lost !

My grandfather dead, my parents moved to a large manufacturing place; and my mother's eldest sister, having no daughters of her own, claimed me for an unlimited time.

If she had put me right into her kitchen, and taught me how to " bake and to brew," I think a good deal of troublesome romance would have gone off in the smoke incident to that useful pastime.

Through mistaken kindness this was not done; and over the intervening years, I solemnly declare *that* kindness to have been the wreck upon which I went down.

Instead of the frying-pan, Algebra !

What need has a girl of Algebra? She spends her money too fast to stop and reckon it.

Instead of the pudding-bag, French!

Was she ambitious to hear me scold my future household in that voluble tongue?

Parents! whatever else you fail to do, learn, betimes, your female offspring TO COOK.

We may have our eating-saloons, our fashionable restaurants, our imported " Blot's ; " but one old style, well-prepared dinner, outweighs them all!

Meanwhile I was put through a course of studies that would have floored any girl, whose mental activity had not been quickened, as mine.

I enjoyed it.

Nature, Art, the Sciences, lay open before me.

Text-books of a high order were at hand.

My education, intellectually, was not neglected.

There is no good, however, without its attendant evil. Here, in this excellent family my very worst characteristic — pride — was secretly fostered; and in its rapid growth, overshadowed many a better quality.

Others looked upon me as something a little uncommon, and I certainly regarded myself in that light.

But for one thing, Eternity will prove me indebted to this pious woman.

My religious faith became so rooted and grounded, that no after shock of temptation or sin could drift me from my Scriptural mooring.

"Among the faithless, faithful she,"

and had her Bible told her the sun did not shine, with her eyes in her head, she would have ignored his rays.

So would I!

From this time a new element was infused into my composition.

Impulsively giving up other pursuits, I

sought to fathom its mysteries; and devoting all my energies to the one study of the
revealed Word, I was led on, fascinated by
the glorious truths, until Religion became
my one idea.

My Aunt in her daily life was an epitome,
a living example of her faith.

I then thought the same divine afflatus
had taken possession of *my* heart.

Possibly it had; and after wanderings
were over the smouldering spark that, by
and by, should flame up, repurifying every
emotion.

CHAPTER V.

THE CIRCUS.

" The rude hall rocks — they come, they come,
The din of voices shakes the dome."

"And hurry, hurry, off they rode
As fast as fast might be."

PLEASURE again claimed me. Home to D——.

The town is all agog!

Upon straggling fences and unused buildings, in the Market Square, and at the Post-office, are enormous hand-bills, setting forth that next Wednesday morning a Circus Troupe will make their entrance. The whole company, in gorgeous costume; splendid horses, with rich trappings; band playing, banners flying. "Afternoon performance to commence at two o'clock, door open at one. Evening performance to commence at seven o'clock, door open at six. Admittance twenty-five cents. Children, accompanied by parents, half price."

It is with the afternoon performance I have to do.

I am quite young; precisely at that age girls are most desirous to look well.

I have a beau; sort of half and half; keeps me on the anxious seat all the time with his indecision, whether to stick by me, or go with Lucy Dean!

I feel that the matter of an extra ribbon would decide him.

It is a settled thing. My mother will not give me money to throw away upon what *she* calls "wicked amusements."

Now I have had my mind all summer interested in a certain blue sash, and have saved up a quarter of a dollar towards buying the same.

If my irresolute friend invites *me*,

"Everything is lovely, and the goose hangs high ; "

but if he should choose that dark-eyed miss, good-by to the sash, for I am going Wednesday afternoon to see that Show.

For once, the weather deserved credit. It was propitious.

" Nor too hot, nor too cold,"

and all the forenoon streams of vehicles — from the stylish carriage, that drove directly to the hotel and deposited its load in care of the obsequious landlord; to the country wagon; that brought wife, children, lunch, and hay for Dobbin to munch, while his companions within were feasting upon the unwonted pageant, — poured through the streets.

Shall I ever forget that day ?

The tent pitched on the open common, so white against the clear blue sky, while from its centre floated the Flag we have all learned since to love. The air so pure, The grass so green. The people in their best clothes. The hurrying hither and thither to accost a friend, or secure a good position. Jokes on every side. The trampling of horses; over all the lively music, together produced a flutter of excitement that told pleasantly upon the nerves, and evoked expressions of good feeling from the most reserved.

The exhibition was advertised at two o'clock. By one every seat was taken; and all the space between the pit and the more elevated boards, filled with a jostling crowd.

I was among the first on the ground, and took my place about half way up; neither so low, but I could see the feet of the performers — neither so high, but I was out reach of sun, wind, or flapping canvas.

Now began the fun!

Loafing men, inside, struggling for a chance.

Loafing boys, outside, eager to get in, but just short of the magic sum wherewith to effect an entrance.

The more daring tried to force their way under the tent. But no sooner were head and shoulders well in, than an unexpected jerk of the leg, at the hand of a watchful "attaché," twitched the poor sinner out.

Pent between two monstrous women — one had a baby in her lap — I looked here and there to discover my acquaintance.

Yes — yonder was my beau, the vacillating! over whom I had cried half the night — flirting and making love to that miserable Lucy Dean.

How homely the girl is!

What *can* William Watson see to fancy in *her?* and, am I to believe my eyes! tied round the awkward creature's waist is my blue sash!

I could tell it among a hundred. I knew my fate hung on *that!*

3

Pride crushed back my tears; and just then, too, with flourish of trumpets, came flying through the narrow alley "The Troupe," to see which I had sacrificed so much.

Was there ever anything so magnificent?

How rich they must be! Crimson velvet dresses, trimmed with gold.

And such horses! even their saddles all over gold!

Where did so much come from? I know. *New York.*

But see them prance!—in and out—in and out! just like a dance. Why! it *is* a dance. The band is playing a waltz.

How glad I am I came! Who cares for Bill Watson, Luce Dean, or the old sash either?

Good gracious! What is that fellow doing?—piling glass bottles to stand upon? so high too! is he stark mad? Suppose the underneath one should happen to *break !*

He has reached the top, and, as the crowd applauds, stretches out his arms!

I shall faint dead away — I know I *shall!*

Now isn't *that* boy a beauty? The man with him must be his father — and they are going to ride one horse. How carefully he holds on to the little chap that he may not fall — and kisses him, two or three times.

What! — the boy has sprung to his feet — is upon his father's hand — upon his father's shoulder — upon his father's head — with both arms and one leg in the air — the horse all the time going round the ring fast as ever he can gallop!

I hold my breath!

I know that tune the band is playing,

" Pretty, pretty Polly Hopkins,"

and the men are laying down a piece of carpet.

Somebody is going to dance!

O! isn't that the handsomest girl that

ever was born? I guess Luce Dean will feel worked up now! her dress is awful short, though! that's the way they wear them in New York; but her feet are just as nice as they can be — and such lovely bronze slippers! her white lace overskirt, caught up on the left side, with a pink rose — pink sash (I am glad I didn't buy that *blue* thing), and pink buds in her hair.

Her partner! isn't *he* sweet? green satin trousers, white silk stockings, black shiny pumps, and a little straw hat on one side, with narrow green streamers.

Now they begin. See their steps!

> "Pretty, pretty Polly Hopkins,
> How do you do? *how* do you do?"

She flies from him! He cannot overtake her! She taps him on the shoulder, and before he can turn, she's gone!

> "Pretty, *pretty* Polly Hopkins!"

What a dance you are leading that enamored swain!

" Now they begin.   See their steps!" — Page 36.

What's *that?* the growl of a lion? They don't have lions at a circus. It can't be *thunder!* When did the shower come up? How it rains! The spectators are leaving. I hope Luce Dean's sash will get wringing wet, and all the color run out, the minx!

O, how it lightens! If I was only at home! Mother said it was wrong to come. I know I shall be struck. Dear me! dear me!

With the vision of

"Pretty, *pretty* Polly Hopkins!"

before my eyes — and, mingling with the thunder, the refrain,

"None the better, Tommy Tompkins,"

in my ears — I rush for the door.

The grand times I had, in that dear old village!

If these pages chance to meet the eye of S. M., K. H., R. W., recall what dances!

made memorable by the wonderfully exe
cuted " Turkey Step " of W. J., and the ap
proving slap of G. I. I. upon his fat legs,
after his well-cut " Pigeon's Wing."

What sleigh-rides in winter ! what beach
rides in summer !

Life now was gala !

It will not be supposed I could take all
these rides with good-looking young men —
enjoy all these dances with well - dressed
beaux, — and come off heart whole !

O, no ! many was the skirmish I had with
the little " god of love ; " and one of his
well-aimed thrusts, took six weeks to heal !

CHAPTER VI.

THE TWICE ELOPED.

"And now is seen the passion for utility, when all things are accounted by their price."

"And she has met with Glenlyon,
Who has stolen her away."

NEVER attempt to dodge your destiny; as well float up current. You cannot do it.

About this time I ran away. As I am romantic, I will express myself differently. *I eloped.* Not in company with a lover, but — with myself!

Two motives induced me. I wanted to see the city — and my dear father's death leaving us in straitened circumstances — I wanted to "turn an honest penny."

Why I did not take to school-teaching

honorable and remunerative, I am unable to tell.

Hiding my light, as it were, under a bushel; unknown to my friends, I entered a leading store as saleswoman.

My world was immediately turned upside down!

My mother's blue blood boiled in her veins!

Her twin sister's son, from the hour I thus ignobly lowered the aristocratic banner of our house, pitiless and unforgiving, walks the streets of Boston, vouchsafing to me no cousinly glance!

Meantime I made a capital clerk.

Algebra told! and many a customer rued the day I had applied myself so closely to its calculations.

I discovered a business talent.

No greater change, however, could possibly have been made in any individual life. Heretofore, mistress of my own time, habits

of a born lady, proclivities decidedly literary. Now, busily employed all day, I had
no opportunity to exercise my tastes or enjoy my books.

But I could study human nature; and,
believe me, there is a good deal of it round!

Better not, ladies! go into a store with
heads so high you can scarcely see the person who serves you. Better not, ladies!
address her as a lower order of creation;
for the girl who ties up your purchase, may
be, in birth and education, immeasurably
your superior.

There *are* those who understand, and, to
their honor, act in accordance; that in the
inexplicable confusion of life, some are jos-
tled out of their sphere.

Fortunately, for my peace of mind, and
lean purse, I did not care for dress; rather
held to the Chinese notion, — *one* thing forever! Still, there were days when I liked
to put on all my finery, and mildly enjoy
the extra notice.

Take it all in all, this was about the happiest period of my life.

Well may I think so !

As then, my Destiny fulfilled her mission, and leading me to my supremest happiness; introduced me to the gifted son of — a Methodist preacher.

From that time existence took on a deeper meaning.

My whole being recognized, and went out to its new master — LOVE — and, welcomed to its resting-place, returned no more ; but dwelt forever there, in sweetest peace.

There are three things that interest the public. Birth ; Marriage ; Death.

They had got well over my birth ; and while waiting for my death, took in hand my marriage.

Obscurity availed nothing. Sensation was my twin sister.

The engagement of the only daughter of Captain E—— to a humble minister's son, was, for the time being, among my acquaintances, the topic.

Methodists, twenty years ago, were not what they are to-day, in either education or popularity.

We will leave the Book of Doom to decide whether, upon *its* unprejudiced pages, as many were not registered favorably then, as now!

Meanwhile, there was a strong counter pressure brought to bear upon the contemplated match by those interested in breaking it off. Foremost among whom was a sheep-faced, inanimate, rival suitor.

If there had been anything wanting to decide the question, this foolish interference would have supplied the link.

Serenely keeping our own counsel, we, the principal faction concerned, accepted one " Thanksgiving " an invitation to dine out. I well remember the dinner. It really was capital!

But it is with heartfelt sadness I record, that one, to whose kindness then, and often after, I was indebted; leaving her earthly friends in sorrow to mourn, now feeds upon the heavenly manna.

Leaving, my companion announced to our surprised hosts, that ere all met again we "twain should be one flesh;" and hurrying to the depot — took the train for Providence, R. I., in those days the "Gretna Green" of persecuted lovers.

Evidently I was getting my hand in — to Elopements!

Arriving there, an unforeseen obstacle presented itself. It was necessary to be "cried;" or, even in that accommodating city, the marriage would not be legal.

"Great oaks from little acorns spring."

That year politics ran high — and even

the good cheer of a regular holiday, could not restrain the zeal of a few souls ardent in the cause.

An excited knot, sufficient in number to form a quorum, was hunted up; and much to their amusement, the Town Clerk published in their ears the " bans of wed-lock," between " contracting parties, Paul Pennington and Elizabeth M. Weymouth, both of Boston, Massachusetts."

The delay over, a willing clergyman ratified the whole thing — not forgetting in the haste to rejoin his feasting family, to dwell at some length upon the word o-b-e-y.

I think I never realized the comprehensive meaning of those four letters, until elaborated by his tongue.

With a generous fee in his hand, *he* went back to the waiting group; and in fluttering happiness, *I* exchanged my maiden freedom for the soft restraint of a blushing bride!

CHAPTER VII.

I AM A WIFE.

" And a well-assorted marriage hath not many cares."

THERE never was a rich Methodist minister!

If lucky enough to receive sufficient salary to keep soul and body together; and fifty cents over for a rainy day; he will inevitably give away the fifty cents.

Rejoicing in a father whose "treasures were laid up in heaven," my husband had his own way to make in the world.

I at once determined to aid him in the laudable undertaking.

I deserve the more credit, as it was done before "strong minded" women came tumbling into the arena; upsetting every blessed man; and seizing, with all else they can lay hands on, their very breeches, so to speak, as trophies of victory!

It was some years before the war, too.

Times then, and the mode of doing busi ness, were quite different. The high pres sure system was not so much the style. A young man of industry and integrity had an almost certain prospect of success. His *word* entered into the account, and if honorably redeemed, was additional capital.

Now, arrangements written in blood are hardly considered binding.

Then, Honesty was a power.

Now, ignored as "behind the times," she hides her diminished head; and, crestfallen, acknowledges "*she don't pay!*"

Then, the aspirant was willing to wait, and receive gifts from Fortune as he earned them. Now, the poor Jade is so "battered and bruised," that — fleeing for her life — she scatters indiscriminately her treasures, and Young America secures the largest share !

" A man is praised as he does well for himself."

1873 indorses the days of Job !

We took a small store. With just one hundred and fifty dollars, started in business.

We were young, healthy, and had our wits about us.

Soon people began to find, indeed it became rather the fashion, to patronize us; and there is not a person living who ever had dealings with Mr. P——, but will bear witness, " his word was as good as a bond."

As for myself — well ! I was more conscientious then, than I am now.

One thing was sure. We devoted our whole time to business. An early hour in the morning — a late hour at night — found us still employed.

I gave up all my acquaintance; or, what

amounted to the same thing, they all gave up me ; and, obedient to my nature, took hold in earnest of the thing in hand, only too happy in the constant companionship of my husband.

All the outside time we could possibly command was devoted to reading, study, and mutual improvement. None given to pleasure.

Influenced by his sedate and consistent life, I again became interested in religion. This second conviction leading me through a heart-rending experience, in which " Satan was determined to sift me as wheat." To his discomfiture, however, I united with the Church ; of which to-day I am its most unworthy member.

Meanwhile in trade, there were the usual ups and downs; until the great financial crisis swept over the land.

Many large houses were completely uprooted. In our snug little quarters we just made out to weather the gale; but it took many a weary month to repair damages.

Time passed on. Increased success was again ours; and, looked upon as " rising," we considered ourselves — established.

CHAPTER VIII.

A PRESENTIMENT.

"The idol of thy heart is, as thou, a probationary sojourner on earth."

IT now became evident that one of the partners must give up — and taking, I think, the respect and good wishes of our customers, I bade adieu to public, and entered upon private life.

Behold me! in a pleasant home, a few miles from the city, invested with the new dignity of housekeeper; the happy mother of a growing family.

My husband, also, made a change.

In a larger building; extending his operations; with tact and shrewdness, slowly but surely, he laid the foundation of a more than competence.

Everything prospered.   His unyielding principle had got him an excellent name. Old firms were pleased to acknowledge the successful, self-made young merchant.

In both business and social relations he was favored.

As I have said, he was religious.   Up to this time he had worshipped with his Congregational brethren.   But now, true to the faith of his fathers, he formed an embryo society — the increasing membership of which — still hold him in grateful memory.

We had lived in M—— about ten years; in as perfect a state of happiness as can well fall to the lot of mortals.

We owned our house.   Its appointments were comfortable, even elegant.   My tastes were all gratified.   My wants all met — and supposing this state of thing would always continue — I lived on.

At the close of this last year, however; indeed, all during the month of Decem ber, I was a prey to the most distressing but persistent fancies.

A great Shadow had fallen upon me!

I became conscious some terrible misfortune was impending.

So entirely did this belief take possession of my mind, that I passed the greater part of each day in tears; often apologizing to friends for the unaccountable emotion, which I could neither explain, nor banish.

It seemed absolutely certain that something awful would occur before the old year died out; and when the new year, bright and glorious, came in; my husband, my children well; the house standing firm on its foundation; words could not express my joy.

But, I was not alone in my Presentiment!

The first day of January, 18—, fell on Sunday.

A reverend gentleman, who was taking

tea with us, upon moving from the table requested permission to kneel.

Thus he prayed —

" We stand upon the threshold of another year. Thanks be to our heavenly Father, all is well. Soon, we may be called to part — child with its parent — parent with its child. Wife with her husband " —

Suddenly he stopped; with the sensation of a blow upon his head; words failed — he could go no farther.

Monday morning dawned. Its peaceful hours went on.

Punctually returning in the six o'clock train, the dear, well-known step in the hall fell upon my ear.

The events of the day discussed; the pleasant evening meal finished; the children — a father's kiss warm upon their rosy lips — fast asleep; my husband commenced reading aloud to me.

All at once, putting his hand to his head,

he exclaimed, "O! this rush of blood!" and giving no sign, fell dead at my feet.

Friends rushed in! Medical aid was summoned!

It was of no avail.

The respected business man — the adored husband — the beloved father — the faithful church member; leaving business, wife, children, *and* church — had gone to his God!

Would I could here stop; lay down my pen; close mine eyes; and join the departed!

But no! Living, I am a widow!

CHAPTER IX.

I AM A WIDOW.

"And I said this in sorrow ; but pity cannot reach it."

" All things being are in mystery."

AT a comparatively early age — I was eleven years younger than I am now — I lost my husband.

I mourned him with my whole soul.

The world appeared dark ; and there was no brightness to relieve my sombre sky.

To do as he would approve became my chief desire.

Naturally, my first efforts were directed towards the struggling, religious society he had left.

Mr. P—— was a Methodist from choice. I, because of the love I bore him.

A witty minister of the "standing order" used to say, "that as fast as I was
twisted into a Methodist at one end, I un-
raveled as a Congregationalist at the
other!"

Be that as it may — I am confident that
had Paul Pennington hailed as a god, the
SUN; rather than have been separated from
him, I should, a devout worshipper of the
same luminary, have knelt by his side.

> "Thou, for my sake, at Alla's shrine,
> I, at any god's, for thine!"

Happily for my future, he had welcomed
the True Light, and his heart was illumined
by divine rays.

Seven is considered the ruling number.

Not so by me!

THREE, comprise the mystic cycle of *my*
fate.

I have passed through *three* distinct
phases of life!

I have had *three* special calls to a relig
ious life!

I have suffered *three* marked punishments for not conforming to that life!

And I have had *three* — separate VISIONS!

Now I am not a Spiritualist. I have no sympathy with this wonder of the nineteenth century. But as regards these, thus evidenced by my senses, the last trump itself will not shake my faith.

One — early in life — when, alone in my chamber; torn asunder with desire to throw myself into the arms of the Saviour; hindered by frightful unbelief from so doing; I saw, with my own eyes — A HAND — extended to help me upwards.

One — later in life — when, again alone; striving to break the iron band of worldliness that held me in its riveted embrace; I heard, with my own ears — A VOICE — earnestly asking me "to give up seeking religion!"

One — latest — when, in a crowded conference meeting; I saw, with my own favored sight — MY HUSBAND — standing, white-robed, with the angels; joining in the song of praise then going up to heaven from his Christian brethren, assembled in evening worship.

But we are all human beings; and though "grief may endure for a night, joy cometh in the morning."

With time, the "great consoler," my feelings were somewhat modified; and assumed a more healthy tone.

I was still young, tolerably good-looking, and at this late day developed a wonderful power "to attract."

I do not think I had ever before realized my capacity in that line. My nature had been too concentrated; in turn, too absorbingly interested in one thing.

To make the most of available "points," it is necessary to generalize, to diffuse.

If that were the condition, clearly I• was on the high-road to success !

Going over soul and body to the other extreme, I generalized; until the whole brotherhood of mankind was embraced in my far-reaching regard.

I diffused; until there was nothing left *to* diffuse.

Heart, house, and purse were thrown wide open, and friends trooped around.

The caution of the elder Weller to his son " Samivel " was thrown to the wind.

A young widow at the head of an establishment, is a mighty taking thing.

People regarded me now with favor, who allowed my " shop girl " era to slip from their memory. Yet I was not nearly as deserving their esteem, prodigally scattering, as when carefully gathering. So goes the world!

" *Revenons à nos moutons.*" Just here comes in the innocent art of cooking.

If, three times a day, I had been obliged to prepare food for my household; for lack of time, the quicksands into which my wandering feet were drawn, would never have been explored.

Our family physician "hit the nail on the head" when he wished "I had not a cent in the world, and six children to clothe and feed." I shrank with horror from the bare idea of what would have proved an Evangel.

He well understood two things ; my organization, and the importance of necessitated employment.

The homely lines —

> "Satan finds some mischief still
> For idle hands to do," —

are very significant. To everybody outside an "oyster," work was the one blessing given when driven out of Paradise.

Unoccupied time is a fearful engine of evil.

Hopkins' hell — paved with the skulls of infants ! Hades — peopled with good resolutions ! are a "*bagatelle*," alongside the thronging multitude sent to the "dark Plutonian shore," as punishment for deeds committed through idleness !

Upon how many tombstones might be truthfully engraved —

"Gone to the Devil; because of — TOO MUCH LEISURE ! "

CHAPTER X.

MY EVIL GENIUS.

"But if thou nourish in thy heart the reveries of passion."

I HAD always the sympathy of the little "society."

My home became, as it were, a grand *rendezvous* for the Methodists. Social gatherings, class and committee meetings, succeeded each other.

I heartily entered into the spirit of them all; and to this day recall them with pleasure.

But no weather stayed the tide. I became alarmed for the well-being of my Brussels carpets; and in a happy moment conceived the idea of confining the "stewards" to an old rug.

I see them before me! planted in a row; full of finance; yet careful, in their greatest excitement, never to allow one foot to go over the prescribed limit.

And the sympathy, too, of one dear old lady; for whom I reserved "a little chamber on the wall," sacred to her own use; who, catching the falling mantle of my sainted aunt, bore me up with her prayers; and — I do not doubt — opened for me a good account with the court of heaven!

I had failed in getting my husband's life insurance.

Not liking the company in which for a number of years he had been insured, he proposed to change. The papers were made out, awaiting the doctor's signature. Pending this, Paul died; and having signified his intention to the old company — neither new nor old felt obliged to put out their money.

Sorry for my loss, a person conversant with the circumstances called to condole.

Was it the dead, come back to explain?

A faintness as of death came over me; but recovering, I entered into conversation. I found him educated, well-bred, a gentleman in every sense of the word.

An external resemblance so striking, could but argue similarity in character.

This fact immediately arrested my attention and interested my feelings.

Could it have been otherwise?

Impulsiveness in youth, is often recklessness in maturer years. I am not conscious of ever having considered an act in connection with its result.

I ought on the spot to have called in Fancy and shut down the gates. I did not do it; and getting the upper hand — she took me rough-shod

"O'er many a brier, and many a brake," —

until with bleeding feet, stripped, peeled, and torn, she has set me down on a barren coast.

5

But I anticipate !

My new friend was religious. This made him the more engaging — as contradictorily — however much I may have followed the Evil, I am powerfully attracted towards the Good.

His sympathetic nature called forth mine. In telling him my troubles, they disappeared. In asking his counsel, I again had a guide. In receiving his instructions, I learned very highly to regard.

All this time I was aware he was married; but having no idea of entering that state myself, the knowledge did not disturb me.

All I asked was sympathy; friendship; these satisfied.

How arrive at these without companionship ?

There was where regret came in heavy upon my soul; and for every hour I detained him from her who had a better right to his society, I have endured months of torture.

"The mills of the gods grind slowly,
But they grind exceeding small,"—

and whoever goes as grist to their mill, is smothered in his own dust!

Everybody needs a change; though it may be from good to bad. It is an unalterable law of our being. Not often understood; seldom acted upon.

If I had now taken a short journey — thereby forcing my feelings into a different channel — the aim would have been accomplished; and I should gladly have come back to my pleasant home.

Just then, too, my brother was continually bringing me into difficulties.

When himself, a better-hearted man never lived; so kind — so useful — that I really felt I could not keep house without him; but, like the cow that gave a good pail of milk, then upset it; the poor fellow in his cups, undid all

He borrowed money of my friends who expected me, in honor, to pay it.

When sober he seldom talked; when in liquor he was all talk — and in his jealous, suspicious moods — got me into more scrapes than I could well manage.

The house filled with company was his opportunity.

I well recollect upon the occasion of a party, missing certain guests; and finding them in a remote room, all the preserves in the pantry before them, "cheek by jowl" with James, with one spoon regaling themselves!

He often, too, attempted to frighten, and in that way get the best of me.

Once, however, I had him at a disadvantage. He was persevering; if he commenced a thing, would be sure to finish. I had a row of poplars I wished cut down and set him to the job. All through those hot summer days he chopped and sawed

sawed and chopped, bored and salted, until every tree was "done for" beyond a hope of resurrection !

Would, as then, my only brother could be with me now !

Altogether I began to grow uneasy, dissatisfied, and tired of everything about me.

Widows of four years' standing will sympathize with me in this. It is uncomfortable to be constantly reminded of lost happiness.

So, without duly considering the subject, I sent for an auctioneer — and sold out !

My house being well furnished, drew a crowd; and seldom had the handsome "Knight of the Hammer" as good an opportunity to display his peculiar eloquence.

It was all over; my life at M—— wound up — and I again a resident of Boston.

In this connection there occurred a singular thing.

The practical is uninteresting. I am eminently practical. I am eminently uninteresting ; but this —

One Saturday night, my small family in bed and wrapt in slumber; I, alone up and wakeful, went into the dining-room and seated myself at a large, black-walnut, extension-table.

With paper before me, pencil in hand, I was summing the probable proceeds of the sale.

The utmost stillness prevailed.

Suddenly, within one inch of the paper, there was a heavy, resounding blow; as though some strong, muscular hand had come down flat on the palm, with all its force.

The " masterly " retreat at Bull Run was a circumstance to my exit from that room; ascent of those stairs ; bolt into my mother's chamber.

I declare, my blood curdles even now as I think of it!

I have stated the fact. I leave wiser heads to account for it.

Only — as the IT, invisible, had shaken my calculations; I wish the IT, visible, had so shaken my bones; that, stiff and sore, flat on my back, unable to move; per necessity, taking time to determine its expediency; I had been saved the first fatal step of breaking up, through the agency of that good-looking auctioneer, my peaceful, comfortable home!

CHAPTER XI.

" Refresh thy jaded limbs, return with vigor to the strife."

FOR a long time I had not boarded; and I thought being summoned to my meals, ushered to my seat, served with rich viands, would be decidedly " the thing."

Hotels *are* pleasant — but my diffusive period had quite put it out of my power to indulge in *that* luxury.

Imagination tided me into a regular boarding-house; second or third rate; I never could make up my mind how to class it.

For a while, novelty served me a good turn. Very slowly the curtain rose, revealing " behind the scenes." " *En passant*," if

it is your fate to board, never go near the
kitchen; if your reason don't fail, your ap
petite will!

Presently I began to be considered an
old boarder. Attentions flagged. Treated
coldly at table, if not on hand when rung
down. Savory morsels all reserved for
newer comers. Innuendoes respecting the
quantity of food consumed by some folks,
and statements as to its price.

I became a perfect "price current."
Could quote all the fluctuations of " Faneuil
Hall Market;" tell to a fraction the cost of
butter — and rise in sugar; when lard was
" steady "— and ashes " quiet."

The romance of boarding was at an end.

Observing how profitably this woman
pulled the ropes; determined she should
pull no more at my expense; and with an
eye to the main chance, I suddenly " bought
out" a house.

A word of caution to my fellow-creatures

about to invest in that most hazardous of all stock, a "*furnished* dwelling-house."

Take up every carpet and examine it against the light!

Sound every dish to certify the cracks!

Sit down in every chair to try their legs!

Sleep on every bed to test its vitality!

If carpets, dishes, chairs, stand the trial; if you rise in the morning safe in wind and limb; haggle no longer, clinch the bargain.

My "bargain" was in a fair part of the city — and eschewing boarders, I let all my spare rooms to lodgers — merely to lodgers!

I believe, now-a-days, it is thought difficult to determine a person's status.

Although I had undergone "an experience" I was most awful green.

My house seemed well filled. The occupants coming to me one after another to ascertain whether they could retain their rooms, and on what terms, appeared satisfied that it had come into my hands.

One thing struck me as a little curious. With a single exception, they were all girls.

Now I had made up my mind to lodge gentlemen; but they were here — so nice and pleasant — and besides, "a bird in hand is worth two in the bush" any day. I could not find it in my heart to send them away.

In putting things to rights, and making them comfortable generally, a week passed on.

I thought I had fallen upon a streak of luck now, sure — and settled myself down for the winter — when lo! the aforesaid "exception," a young man, appeared; and requested an interview.

All honor to that young man!

Be he what he may — be he where he may — I thank him!

He asked me if I understood the nature of my house, and the character of its in-mates?

Perceiving that I did not comprehend, he went on to inform me, "that I was at the head of a first-class 'fancy' establishment; with a first-class set of kept mistresses under my immediate charge."

Transfixed with horror, I heard him through.

They had been deceived by the retiring landlady.

I was not what they supposed.

His conscience would not suffer me to be kept in the dark another day. Under seal of secrecy he made the *exposé*, leaving me at liberty to act as I thought proper.

It was midnight!

Falling flat to the floor, I passed the night in an agony of thought.

To clear the house was, of course, a foregone conclusion.

But what would my friends say? my mother? my child?

O God! if thou hadst not sustained me through that fearful suspense ——

Morning dawned. If never before — nor
never since — *that* day I saw the sun rise;
and by nine o'clock there was not a soul on
the premises save myself and the astonished cook.

I was smothered! I could not breathe!
rushing, I threw windows and doors wide
open, to let in all of Heaven's pure air.

I had been to a great deal of expense.
The place was in fine order. However, *I*
could not enjoy it — and selling at a sacrifice — I was once more afloat!

CHAPTER XII.

THE QUIET TOWN OF L——.

"Seekest thou rest, O mortal? seek it no more on earth."

"Man, thou hast a social spirit."

DISGUSTED with my city experiences, I sought a more tranquil sphere; and accordingly withdrew from " the haunts of men " to the quiet town of L——.

I still felt alone. Amid all, my heart was continually thrown back upon itself to consume its own vitality.

From year to year I became more and more unhappy. Every change seemed for the worse.

Shall it be the same with this last?

The few friends I had in the place tried to make it agreeable — but their efforts not

being met half-way, were discontinued —
and life was at a dead lock.

Better had it forever remained so!

I had one accomplishment which now
came into play.

I sewed well.

That I had been early taught to do; and
as a child, it had been no small gratification
to hear friends praise my beautiful stitches.

Sewing is a safety-valve! many a disor-
dered fancy passes off at the point of the
needle. I always pitied the sterner sex for
this, their great deprivation.

But they have their cigars! and smoke is
useful!

With all my improvidence, I was eager
to earn; and so pressed this gift into the
service.

I made shirts — fine shirts — for gentle.
men; and the opportunity given; as in the
case of a young friend; I have no doubt I
too, could have secured a good husband, if

I had wanted one, through the agency of " custom sewing."

I presume my power of " attraction " con. tinued in full force.

I judge so, from the many professions of undying love poured into my listless ears.

I did not wish to marry. It was suggested, that after such a lapse of time, to change my condition would be more than proper; I, however, did not care to. That was enough.

Even my strong craving for sympathy had somewhat abated.

The fact was, I had now got thoroughly interested in my *shirts!*

I received them from an establishment where they were manufactured to order; and have often wondered if my male acquaintance, in slipping on their well-fitting garment, dreamed whose fingers had put it together! or whether, when we met, they noted the close scrutiny to which they were subjected, in my desire to see if the "plaits" were all right!

.

"There is no peace for the wicked!" Less for a widow!

In this secluded place my Evil Genius again turned up, and planted itself directly in my path; this time also, in the question able shape of — another married man!

What was up?

Had I to make good the deficiencies of my wedded female friends?

In some cases, the task would be too Herculean.

In this, I did not make the attempt: but I must here confess; the good looks, the good heart, the evident *penchant* of the gentleman, excited an interest — and perchance would have made a deeper impression — had I not previously been ground to . powder for the very same offense; thinking

6

a little too much of a man, sworn to another!

Experience is a very costly, but a very good teacher, where it does not come too late.

I am indebted to it — and have written on the most obscure leaf of my private diary — IF married again, look sharp to your husband; and put no faith in that arrant humbug — *sympathy!*

CHAPTER XIII.

THE FATES.

"That I may see once more
The splendor of the setting sun
Gleam on thy mirrored wave."

" And thou Lachesis
Dost spin the thread of human life !"

MONTREAL! Grand in its churches! Its convents! Its religious processions! Its situation !

Whoever has courage to ascend the turret of " *Notre Dame* " — fifteen feet higher than our own Bunker Hill Monument — is richly repaid in a charming panoramic view of the city at his feet.

Spanning the St. Lawrence, is the far-famed Victoria Bridge; and the noble river itself, with many an island lying upon its calm bosom.

As I write, memory vividly recalls the happy hours passed upon its waters; the fear of its dangerous rapids being lost in admiration of the scenery along its shores.

Here, too, occurs this singular phenomenon — the Ottawa and St. Lawrence flowing side by side — each retaining its distinctive color.

Montreal, Americanized as it is, presents in itself and its surroundings so much of the foreign and picturesque, that each season beholds its streets thronged with travellers seeking the cool, invigorating air; together with the thousand objects of interest claiming attention at every step.

And artists — endeavoring to transfer to canvas the mountain, crowned to its top with foliage; through which, glimpses may be caught of a winding road gay with vehicles of every description; from the youthful occupants of which — it would require but little stretch of the imagination —

music and laughter are borne back upon the wind!

Neither does he forget the low, quaint cottage, adjoining the splendid mansion; each conspicuous by contrast.

Nor the curious costumes; making in appearance, grandfathers and grandmothers of the young: but which delusion is instantly dispelled by the brilliant eye, seen nowhere out of Italy, save in the Canadian born peasant.

Summer has gone! Winter approaches! Travellers and artists hie them to more congenial climes. Ice is formed! The waters of the St. Lawrence congeal. Snow descends! The mountain trees bend beneath its weight.

It piles the streets so high, that from opposite windows, neighbors can scarcely see one another.

Unbroken in its depth — unstained in its whiteness — it lay the whole distance between this great city of " Our Lady," and the obscure, unknown village of Laprairie.

The small houses are far apart!

How, in case of sickness?

A watchful Providence is above all; and has in equal remembrance, the favored inhabitant of the city, the lone dweller in the hamlet.

Thus it came to pass — though the storm raged, and the wind blew round the isolated house — that mingling with its blasts, angels heard the tiny wail of a new-born infant; a mother thanked God her agony was over — a father clasped to his heart — a son!

Of foreign birth, proud of his ancestry, one of whom, high in rank, had fought under the first Napoleon; exclusive in his feelings, naturally and by force of education; Monsieur Chaudet, induced by the prospect of more easily acquired wealth, came to the Canadas; intending eventually to make the " States " his home.

But a " winsome " maiden interfered with his plans ; and settling down —

"Far from the busy haunts of men " —

his wife, his books, his fields, engaged his attention, until a new ambition was aroused by the birth of the little Gustave.

Very early in life the child discovered a nature sensitive to the last degree.

Each influence, for the time being, entirely swayed him ; and the transition from good to bad — or from bad to good — was so instantaneous and so complete, that it was amazing one identity could display such conflicting phases.

That the boy might have educational advantages and mingle with his fellows, the quiet country was exchanged for the bustling city. Laprairie — for Montreal.

Here, witnessing frequent military parades, he acquired a taste for display; and although placed under immediate care of the most self-denying Catholic order; the very ritual of their church — accompanied by its bewildering music — so cultivated in him the æsthetic, that no Parsee adored his burning god, as the young Gustave — "the Beautiful!"

His disposition was generous. His heart tender. His talents of a high order.

Under a father's judicious training there might have resulted, from these several characteristics, a perfect whole.

To the irreparable loss of the son, the . father — hardly entered upon middle life — was suddenly cut down.

And Gustave — the gifted, the tender-hearted, the generously disposed, the easily influenced to good or bad; an orphan, beside himself with grief — was thrown at an early age upon the world, to receive its impress of virtue or vice, as his all important "first step" should determine.

CHAPTER XIV.

LA MAISON DE MAUVAISE FÂME.

"And the wages of her sin shall be hereafter.'

" Look again on this fair girl."

A LARGE house, brown-stone front, in a fashionable quarter of the city.

It was evening.

The street was brilliant with gas.

Only a close observer, however, could have detected lights within the mansion. Heavy draperies thoroughly screened the windows. At intervals alone, a curtain suddenly raised, and as immediately dropped, gave a glimpse of the magnificence within.

In truth, everything wealth could command was to be seen and enjoyed there.

Carpets, so soft the footfall left no echo.

Furniture, gorgeous in its appointments without regard to cost.

Pictures, selected with evident care and taste.

And mirrors, from floor to ceiling reflecting back this beauty, apparently doubled the size of the already spacious apartment.

The hall was dimly lighted. From time to time as a person entered, the door was hastily opened, and at once carefully closed.

Well-dressed were they who ascended those steps. To be envied, in that they were Fortune's favorites — and possessed the "Open Sesame" to even that aristocratic dwelling ; the pass-word to which was — money !

"Ho, there ! wine for a dozen !" peremptorily called a young man to a retreating waiter — as he threw himself into a seat before a marble table, somewhat apart from the other occupants of the room.

" Lor ! massa ' Gus ' — you ain't goin' for to drink all that ar wine, your own self ? " asked the negro, answering the order as directed.

" Never you mind. Clear out ! — and don't show your woolly head till called for — but be mighty sure you are on hand then ; " impatiently responded the individual thus addressed.

" Goin' it strong for a young un ; guess he can't stand all that ar liquor an' keep his eyes peeled ; " muttered the darkey as he closed the door.

Rising, the youth crossed the room ; and with " Come on, Dick ! have a drink ? " seized a comrade by the arm and dragged him over to his table.

" Ha ! French blood 's up ! jealous, by Jove ! won't let me finish my talk with the pretty Louise ! Don't want anybody but yourself round ! If that 's your go — better take her away from here — or you won't have her long. See! another has already got my place. Harris — that rich, old swell — by all that's good! A seat longside *that* girl don't get cold, you bet!"

The. taunting words were unheeded. For making the same discovery, Gustave had pounced upon the girl called " Louise," and fairly lifting her out the circle of her admirers, had carried — as he would have a babe — the slight figure, and set her down close by himself.

It was done so suddenly there was no opportunity for resistance.

"That's too bad!" exclaimed the person thus deprived of his fair companion; directing a fierce glance at his bold rival. " Just the cut of that young scamp, how do you call him? Always takes exactly what one wants, without so much as saying, ' By your leave!' ' There is honor among thieves!'"

" What's that about thieves?" interrupted Gustave. " Look sharp to your tongue, my fine fellow, if you don't want it pulled out by the roots! All is fair in war you know!"

"I say, Harris! why make a ——— fool of yourself? The girl don't care a snap for *you*, anyhow — and they say she's bewitched with that fiery chap's black eyes! Console yourself! — my boy — console yourself! 'There's as good fish in the sea as ever came out of it.' Now here's "—

" ——— if you want to console yourself, do it! But I swear! *I* am not going to submit to anything of this kind. We are six to one, and have Louise I will!"

"Take her if you can get her," remarked Gustave, quietly sipping his wine; at the same time bringing all the fascination of his dark eyes to bear upon the lovely female at his side. "Take her if you can get her"—— and raising his glass to his lips — "Here is to your success, gentlemen!

"'He who wins shall wear.'"

" Then, by Heaven, you French devil ! *I* will wear.   Come on ! " and with one bound clearing the space — Harris had his hand almost upon the girl's shoulder — who, half dead with fright, clung trembling to her companion.

Almost — but not quite. For Gustave, throwing her from him — eyes blazing with fury — sprang to his feet!

Maddened by rage he drew his revolver, - - and the next moment would have been Harris' last, had not the woman — with the instinctive devotion of her sex — flung herself fainting upon the breast of the man she loved — and stayed back his hand from the terrible crime.

The uproar now became general.

Crazed with passion and drink, oaths and curses came thick and fast; and blows too — some of which fell heavily upon tenderly reared forms — all unused to such treatment.

Murder, after all, would inevitably have

closed the scene — but for the timely appearance of the " Madam " of this stylish hell, — who with the warning, " Gentlemen! the police are upon you!" quickly cleared the room — by passing them through a secret passage into the next — outwardly, highly respectable, brown-stone front!

Dick, who during the entire fracas had taken the best possible care of himself, had gone with the crowd.

Gustave, the chief actor, had resumed his seat and again addressed himself to his wine.

He was alone with the girl.

The excitement under which he had labored all the evening, passed away. His voice was low and tender.

" Drink, Louise!" filling high her glass, and touching it to his own lips ere he offered it to his companion ; "drink, ' *mignonne!* ' nothing like wine to drown trouble, — and you and I both need it — for, to-night we part!"

The girl raised her eyes to his in an agony of doubt!

He answered their mute appeal.

"Yes, Louise! we must part. The shadow of life has fallen upon me. I came here purposely to drink, as I never did before, that the very recollection of grief might be taken out of my soul. But it is of no use " — and bowing his head upon his hand — he wept convulsively.

She watched him with intensest interest; at length, laying her delicate hand upon his dark hair, timidly murmured — "Dearest! there is something beside wine to drown trouble — there is love!"

Her voice took on a beseeching tone.

"Take me out of this place. O, Gustave! carry me far away, where no familiar eye shall see me; and — all your own — let me, your Louise, be the one to bring you back to happiness?"

The youth raised his head, and gazed

" Laying her delicate hand upon his dark hair." — Page 96.

. long and earnestly upon the beautiful pleader.

" No, '*mignonne*,' it cannot be. I am not ungrateful. I shall bear with me till my latest hour the remembrance of what you have saved me from this night, but to-day the knowledge came to me that I am an orphan, and penniless.

.. " Nor shall *you* remain here. In the pure atmosphere of your distant home, by re-pentance, you shall atone for our sin of the past few months."

She scarcely heeded his words.

She threw herself before him, and lay moaning at his feet. She entreated. She implored. In vain; and the dread convic-tion fastened upon her that she saw to-night— for the last time, — the face of him she had loved " not wisely, but too well l "

At last, worn out with fatigue and sorrow, Gustave threw himself upon a sofa and slept.

Turning down the lights, Louise, kneeling by his side until break of day, watched with the unsleeping vigilance of love, every movement of the handsome sleeper.

Ah, Gustave! impulsive, misguided Gustave! dost thou thus redeem the ambitious hope of thy dead father for thee, his eldest born?

Ah, Louise! devoted, unhappy Louise! would thy tears, thy prayers had availed; and that he, upon whom thou lavished the deepest affection, had returned thy love; had met the cravings of thy fond heart!

So wouldst thou have been saved.

So would I have escaped the misery that was to result from meeting, in the future, one of whose very existence I was as yet in such blissful ignorance.

CHAPTER XV.

"Thy father's friend, and thine, who tendereth thee tried love."

"By Heaven! I am in luck. St. Louis, too, has a free lunch!

"I say, Charley! what an institution this is!

"How would a poor devil of a fellow manage just now if she hadn't? every cent gone, not a place to put my head. No matter. Food before sleep, and I *am* starved — that's a fact. A shame too, with that rich uncle of mine, for my father's son to be walking the street in this shape!"

"Uncles don't help. Keep up good courage, Gustave. Better times ahead. If I had a dollar in the world, you should have half. Come! you are too good-looking a fellow to be down in the mouth. Pluck up! and walk right straight into the affections of some rich girl, and your everlasting fortune's made without any further bother. All I'll charge you for the idea is — let me see? — you may set me up!"

"What in? — food, or liquor? — the last I judge, from the way you handle it — but remember, the 'drinks' have got to be paid for!"

"Yes — I know; but take a glass; it will give you strength to look up your fortune — the girl — eh, Gustave!"

"No, I will eat; *that* is free — and I shall be ashamed to come here to-morrow — so must lay in a stock while I can."

"Well! good-by — give us your hand! — and be sure you take my advice. I declare 'Gus,' — I feel as good as behind my bar — now!"

The two young men separated.

One, to walk the streets in absolute want. Not a cent in his pocket; long distance away; what should he do? Walk forever? No — his mind is made up; his dinner was given him — his lodging, he will beg.

" But for the love of Heaven, landlord ! — only for the night. Just think ! — for over a week I have not slept in a bed. I am completely worn out. Rest assured I will pay you soon as I can earn the money."

" Lots say the same thing. But I'm a tender-hearted chicken — and you're an honest-looking fellow — so I suppose I'll have to take your word this time.

" Look here, Captain ! see how I'm continually bamboozled into harboring these young people who will pay me when they get work. If half they promise comes in, I shall be a rich man ! "

The individual thus addressed, turned. No sooner had his eye fallen on Gustave, than — seizing him with both hands — he held him in a hearty embrace.

" *You* here! — the son of my old friend begging a night's shelter ; why, how 's this? — landlord! I'll take this young gentleman off your hands.   Thought I recognized the voice — precisely like your father's — don't speak — know all about his death — and it shall go hard if I don't find you a good berth, for his sake.   Got one on hand now, by Jove!   How would you like to be clerk — Captain's clerk — of the good, staunch steamboat *Isabel*, all the way from here to New Orleans? "

The young man overcome by his feelings, could hardly trust himself to reply; and when taking out his purse, the Captain handed him seventy-five dollars — his first month's pay in advance — with the kind remark, " You youngsters are always out of money, and you may need this," Gustave could restrain himself no longer, but burst into a flood of tears.

His affairs had now taken so unexpected and favorable a turn, that he entirely forgot his Mentor, Charley's advice ; thereby ousting that free-hearted young person out of his prospective bar ; and taking the risk of losing a rich wife, he accepted on the spot the generous offer of his father's friend.

CHAPTER XVI.

THE "ISABEL."

"I know a maiden fair to see,
Take care ! "

" I would that I could utter
My feelings without shame ;
And tell him how I love him,
Nor wrong my virgin fame."

" And he that would say
A pretty girl nay " —

AND the Captain's clerk liked his berth.

To be sure, he had a good deal to look after — with considerable responsibility for one so young — and what was new to him, a " gang " entirely under his direction.

But he had already seen something of the world, and felt quite equal to meeting this increased demand upon his ability.

The negro element was his especial enjoyment; and they came fully as much to appreciate him.

In the frequent stops of the *Isabel* to load and unload, Massa " Gus " as they invariably called him, could get the allotted amount of work out of them with less driving than had been their wont.

It is barely possible they had an eye to the extra whiskey which they would be sure to get, if they gave satisfaction to their young master.

There was plenty of excitement, too, connected with the life; constantly "taking on " and " letting off " passengers at the different stations; for somehow the *Isabel* this particular season proved to be the most popular boat on the river.

And when regular duties were over, company, cards, and dances whiled many an hour of the passage up and down the Mississippi.

" What the deuce has got into the women, ' Gus,' this summer ? " sung out the Captain. " Have they all taken to travelling for a living ? *I* never carried so many before in any one year, by Jove ! as I have the last four months. I believe it 's you — with those devilish black eyes — you young rascal ! that 's bewitched them all. Well — go ahead — it 's good for the boat ! "

Gustave with a smile turned away; being pretty sure in his own mind that in some instances it certainly was, either himself, or his " eyes."

In one, he might have sworn to the fact.

On a never-to-be-forgotten evening, as it afterwards proved, being short of a hand at Euchre, they had called as usual upon the young clerk.

His partner was a lady he had never seen before.

She was well-dressed and handsome; very agreeable, and remarkably self-possessed.

She was alone on the " trip ; " and in that way the accidental meeting at the card-table, resulted in a more intimate acquaintance.

By the time she reached her destination it was quite evident that the " black eyes " had done their. usual execution ; and that the stranger had left with their owner — her heart.

This flirtation would like many others, in time, have passed from his mind ; if, as the Captain said, the person in question had not persistently taken " to travel."

Every few weeks she made the passage ; always alone ; and each time, making no attempt whatever to disguise her feelings, became more decided in her advances upon Gustave.

" She showed him the way ; and she showed him the way,
She showed him the way to woo."

It now began really to look as though he would be obliged to marry the lady to get rid of her. The case was desperate. He consulted his friend, the Captain.

"Do no such thing," was the blunt reply "you are too young.   Ship her!"

As his affections were in no wise entangled — and he had other plans for his future — that decided the question; and intimating as delicately as possible the exact state of the case, he supposed, poor fellow, he was well quit of the whole thing.

Once, he had broken off " an affair " — it made his very heart ache to recall that — but then he was not to blame; he could not marry *her*.

This however, he was not destined so easily to dismiss.

CHAPTER XVII.

ANITA.

Abra was ready ere I named her name,
And when I called another Abra came."

" She can both false and friendly be.
Beware! Beware!"

FOR some time Gustave saw no more of his would-be love, Anita.

Finally, towards the close of the season, she came on board to make the "up trip" accompanied by a gentleman, whom she introduced as her brother.

They were to be a while in St. Louis, and hoped often to have the pleasure of meeting Gustave.

As the lady appeared to have given up all designs upon his liberty — and the gentleman appeared to be a genial, polite man of the world—nothing could have been more agreeable than this proposition to the Captain's clerk.

When the boat landed—and Anita escorted to her hotel—the two new friends strolled about the city; regaling themselves as young men will, with a cigar there, a drink here.

It occurred to Gustave that the stranger was particularly attentive, urging him not to spare the wine; and once he thought—but it was so quickly done—if at all—that he immediately dismissed the base suspicion from his mind.

At length Walter proposed going to look up his sister; and took his companion, nothing loth, along with him.

Finding Anita rested, and already seated in the carriage preparatory to taking a drive, her brother instantly placed himself beside her; calling upon Gustave to do the same ; and all were rapidly whirled off.

The walk, the ride, or perhaps the wine he had drank in such unusual quantities, began to make themselves felt.

Silent, Gustave was glad to lean back at his ease; and if not asleep, was at least in that dim, unconscious state, in which the senses scarcely comprehend what is going on around.

"Anita, *mía!* you have got him now — sure — fast enough. A fine scrape! to bring your brother into, just as he has trav· elled half over the world to see you once more. Yes — a devilish fine scrape! What if the authorities get hold of the affair? — where am I? — and you too — sister mine — answer me that? Now in Italy " —

"Hush, Walter! not a word. My life's happiness shall be your reward. We are all that is left to each other. You would not see your sister die before your eyes! — and I tell you again — O, my brother! life, without Gustave — my heart's idol — I will not accept.   But have we not arrived at our destination ? "

" I hope so; for really I begin to feel skittish! Suppose your handsome lover should prove rebellious; and refuse outright the felicity of calling you — my pretty —his bride; what then ? "

" Didn't you use the powder as I told you?   O, Walter! "

"Yes! yes! Don't look at a fellow so! It is all right; if we can only keep him under its influence long enough to get through this confounded job.   You ought to live in Italy.   Your blood is too hot for this part of the world!   *There* you could try your hand at the drug business — and no questions asked — but thank the gods, we are here !   In a few moments I shall salute you as the *cara sposa* of the man you have risked your life, and mine, to obtain; and then, poor me! over the water — alone — never more to see my darling Anita ! "

The carriage stopped.

The lady and her brother alighted.

Gustave followed mechanically; still under the influence of a powerful narcotic.

" Hurry up! or we shall be too late after all; " whispered Walter, as he handed his sister up the steps.

They were evidently expected; and immediately ushered into a room — where the one occupant, a clergyman, prepared for the occasion — was all ready to receive them.

No time was lost in performing the short ceremony, which united for life the young girl to the almost unconscious man at her side.

8

CHAPTER XVIII.

.

THE CAPTAIN'S CLERK.

"In himself ambition is dead."

"Or, if there 's vengeance in an injured heart,
And power to wreak it."

"WHAT! Gustave! my clerk! gone and got married, without so much as telling me, his friend, and his father's friend before him? By Jove! there is some mistake, landlord. 'Gus' wouldn't serve *me* such a slippery trick!"

"He didn't *go* and get married, as I have told you over and over again. Somebody took and married him. Don't you remember that tall girl — with all that hair — who went up and down the river with you so often last summer?"

"Yes — of course I do!"

.

"Well! that's the one. They say she was crazy after your clerk. So she, and her scapegrace of a brother — just got home from one of his long tramps — fixed it all up; and the *rope is spliced!* — tight, too — looked out for that — minister's all regular — and the girl has got her certificate to show for it."

"By Jove! that's outrageous! what I call a true blue 'out-an'-outer.' But, where is 'Gus?' can't spare *him*, married or single."

"You'll have to do it, Captain! It seems by his own account he was drugged; and when he came to and saw how matters stood — he swore he wouldn't live with his wife — no, not an hour; and took an awful oath — that he'd leave no stone unturned — till the cursed knot was untied."

"Poor fellow! I must hunt him up Where did you say he was? It won't do to leave him alone to bear all this load!"

"He's gone off; and you won't see him

round these parts in a hurry, Captain, I tell you!"

"Sorry. I always knew 'Gus' was a brick — and — by Jove! — I glory in his spunk. What has become of the girl!"

"O, her precious brother looked after *her*, poor thing! It was as much as he could do though, to keep her from taking her own life; said she couldn't and she wouldn't live without her dear Gustave. Finally, they got her into the carriage and took her home. I kind of pity her, after all. She's a mighty handsome piece, and has always had her own way!"

It was as our old friend, the landlord, said. Gustave had indeed gone off — nobody knew where.

He had made inquiries, and ascertained that more difficulties than he supposed, lay in the way of untying the "cursed knot," as he styled his forced marriage.

The whole thing was legal — with the ex ception of. his strange statement that he had been drugged. *That* he must prove. There was but one witness — the brother to the bride. He would not be likely to implicate himself, or his sister.

So the whole matter rested; and the be- trayed man — too sensitive to face his old associates — thrown out of his situation, had nothing to do but execrate his fate, or his " eyes," which had brought him into his present unhappy condition.

CHAPTER XIX.

THE GRAND ITALIAN OPERA.

" Tell me, daughter of taste, what hath charmed thine ear in music ? "

THE theatre was ablaze with light!

Carriage after carriage deposited its load of beauty, fashion, and wealth at its door.

Boston's favorite Opera was to be rendered by Boston's favorite artists — and everybody susceptible to the silvery sweetness of Brignoli's " Miserére," or the haunting melody of Phillips' " Prison Song " — was present.

From parquet to ceiling was one living mass of brilliant and interested spectators.

I recall the depreciatory remark of the great Schiller; that a Grand Opera is the

" High up in the crowd stood a slight, but well formed man." — Page 119

auto-da-fé of Nature; yet, always to me —
the rustle of silk, the sheen of satin, the
costly lace, the flash of jewel; the happy
faces, the subdued laughter, the murmur of
voices, the restless motion of graceful forms,
with subtle perfume of the many flowers —
are fitting accompaniments to the impas-
sioned, entrancing melody falling upon the
ear, and hushing every other sound by its
wondrous spell: falling upon the heart, and
stirring in its depths longings, O, such irre-
pressible longings, for the Unseen, for the
Infinite!

High up in the crowd stood a slight, but
well-formed man; rather above the medium
height. That he was young, both face and
figure disclosed.

Graceful in attitude, he was now gazing
intently upon the Prima Donna, oblivious
to all save the ravishing strains she was
pouring forth.

His hair was of the darkest dye, and so thick as partially to conceal his face. Beard he had none; but his full, black mustache, hiding his entire upper lip, gave character to a mouth otherwise rather feminine.

His eyes — but wait! — until the music ceases; and the cheering of the " house " — breaking the spell — causes him to raise them. Ah! in color they match his hair — in size and brilliancy they rival the Italian songstress'.

But soft and tender as they now seem, one instinctively shrinks from the lurking demon detected there, instantly suggesting —

"Land of the Cypress and Myrtle."

He is alone. Speaks to no one. Recognizes no one.

At length, his attention is arrested by two ladies — both evidently past their youth — who are eagerly discussing between the acts the respective merits of their favorite singers, and favorite operas.

The younger, after a while, apparently acquiesces in the superior musical knowledge of her companion; and they again settle themselves to listen.

The young man from time to time regards them.

His eyes seek oftenest the face of the elder.

He would be puzzled to give the reason; as there is nothing at all observable in her appearance.

Her plain dress serves but as a foil to the more gayly attired. Eyes of an uncertain hue — complexion, neither dark nor light — but mantled with the glow of health. She is now in repose; her whole being is absorbed.

But as he looks, those doubtful eyes flash with expression; teeth even and white, gleam between the parted lips; color deepens; and through the master passion of her soul — MUSIC — the woman before him, transformed, is beautiful!

Thus they met! He the younger. She the elder.

CHAPTER XX.

L'INCONNU.

" Whence, and what art thou ? "

THE Opera, successfully inaugurated, lengthened into a season of five or six weeks.

A mutual acquaintance, Fate's chosen instrument, bridged over the separating chasm with the formal introduction —

" Allow me the pleasure, Mrs. Pennington, to present, I hope to your very favorable notice, my particular friend, Monsieur Gustave Chaudet! "

This gave the opportunity which each — unconsciously destined to influence the other for all time — improved.

We both equally appreciated the " divine

art;" and every evening found us its "most constant worshipper."

From casual glances — resulted smiles; slight recognitions; occasional remarks.

I passionately loved music. So intensely indeed, as often to sit with closed eyes, that no attendant "stage" circumstance · might distract from the harmony itself.

Still, I will confess it lent additional interest that the handsome Unknown, night after night, eagerly awaited my entrance to conduct me to a seat.

He appeared quite as much pleased to have fallen in with some one in sympathy with *his* tastes — and who whiled with pleasant talk the expectant moments — before the "rising of the curtain" and "between the acts."

Music is a wonderful medium for the "tender passion;" and of those very sensitive to its power, holds — at times — the Fate!

Thus we, upon the opening night complete strangers — before the last came round — were far on the way to an intimate friendship.

Meanwhile the stranger had ingratiated himself, and narrated many incidents of his romantic life.

He earnestly begged permission to call at my residence; as my society, he assured me, had now become essential to his happiness; and few days passed that some of its hours were not brightened by his presence.

It is generally thought there can be but little sympathy, no love, between the sexes — unless well mated in point of age — *years* being the received data.

I cannot answer for others — and will frankly own — I had never known of but one happy connection where this discrepancy was marked.

When thinking upon this subject at all

serious objections to spending my life with a person so much younger, of course presented themselves.

But I was peculiar; in that, *late* in life *I* had developed; thus bringing my feelings to a level with *his*, my junior — who, thanks to certain "*evénements*" — had on the other hand, matured very *early*.

So that, after all, throwing out of the account what was *in our case* absolutely incommensurate time; we met on the common ground of high health, high spirits, and — inevitable consequence — a mutual fondness for high life.

Friends, alarmed for the result — with the usual success attached to those little "episodes" — interfered.

Although it seemed even at the time, to my own self, inexplicable how it could come to pass; the cravings of my lonely heart *were* really satisfied; and — a shining proof of Folly attempting to cope with Destiny

— I was left to desire no other companionship.

We travelled. Beheld with our own eyes
the grandeur of mountain scenery.

Saw for ourselves the vast, old ocean;
and listened long, to its eternal, solemn ca-
dence.

Looked together upon enchanting land-
scapes; and through the æsthetic our hearts
were powerfully drawn out, and attracted
towards, each other.

My friend made the most extravagant professions of love; and those professions I
had no reason to think otherwise than sincere.

But all this while there appeared to be
a mystery hanging over his life.

Of his past, I knew nothing; save what
he had chosen to impart. I was perfectly
convinced, however, that something — and
of a serious nature too — had been with-
held.

He became fitful. At times, giving ful rein to excitement — fearfully wild; then the reaction — and he was equally gloomy In both phases evidently the victim to un happy memories, which, in spite his best endeavor, would obtrude.

I sought in vain to penetrate the veil.

In the kindest manner — but decidedly — he would invariably put me off; until I became nearly as miserable as himself, and deplored the hour we met.

He had never spoken of marriage — which was singular — as the most casual observer could see that his life's fruition lay at my disposal.

"Tous les jours je t'attends; tu reviens tous les jours,
Est-ce moi qui t'appelle et qui règle ton cours ?"

This state of things could not continue.

A *dénouement* was at hand.

In the course of travel we found our selves at the delightful city of G———.

I had that day privately determined to

bring matters to a crisis; and unless I could satisfactorily fathom the secret, then and there, end the acquaintance.

I obtained his promise to reveal all. But upon the very eve of disclosure his heart failed him, and the revelation was again postponed.

Feeling now positive that indeed there was something of a frightful nature concealed; I demanded to know the worst, however crushing that worst might be.

By way of answer, he displayed to my horror-stricken eyes a poison; which he declared should terminate his existence, if the interview resulted as he feared.

In the face and eyes of this threat, I still insisted; and unable longer to oppose my pleadings — with hesitating voice, tearful eyes, breaking heart — he spoke of his deep love, of his terrible conflict between incli-nation and duty, and confessed; that with

9

all his affections centred in me, he was the bound husband to another!

Though I tore out my quivering heart; honor compelled instantly to banish from my very thought the man who had so entwined himself around its every fibre; and leaving him to bear his own misery as best he might, I went from his presence — forever!

CHAPTER XXI.

AN INTERVIEW.

" What concentrated joy or woe in blest or blighted love ! "

" Scorn me as you will, you are still my husband! I risked reputation — almost life itself — to call you mine; and never, while I breathe, shall another bear your name ! "

" For the last time I ask you. Anita! give me my freedom ? "

" Not that, Gustave ! — all else in heaven and earth ; but not that. Would you drive me insane ? "

" You were already mad when, to accomplish your purpose, you committed the fiendish act. O, but you were cunning! No witness save your brother, as to the manner in which you entrapped me."

"Gustave! It was love that drove me to it. O, forgive me! Take me once to your heart. Look! on my bended knees I swear I never loved another. Every pulsation is for you, and you alone. Devotion such as mine, cannot fail in time to win your tenderness. Grant me that time? By all your hopes of future happiness do not, Gustave, do not — refuse me now!"

"Anita! I came here for no scene — simply to obtain my release; but since you deny me justice, hear what I say! As you love me, so love I another; and had not my honor prevented — in her ignorance of my great wrong — she would to-day have been my wife."

"And you dare tell me this! *Never* will I grant your request. So help me God! I am your wife. As you will not permit me to be your Happiness, I will be your Misery. Go where you will; with whom you will; as your Evil Genius, I shall be forever at your side!" 　.

" Then be the blood of your brother upon your own head, Anita! By Heaven! dead or alive, *he* shall be made to confess; for— I will be free!"

Before she could find words to reply, he was gone; and terrified, lest he should put his threat in immediate execution, she rushed from the room to warn her sick brother; who, upon a sick-bed, was, alas! doomed by a Word more potent than any could be uttered with mortal lips!

CHAPTER XXII.

WALTER.

"But now the hand of fate is on the curtain,
And gives the scene to light."

" You surely would not betray me, Walter! your only sister! who has known no other love than yours from infancy?"

"Anita! I cannot die with this fearful sin on my soul. Think of it! the life's happiness of the young man destroyed; not through fault of his — but yours — and mine."

" To save *him*, must *my* name be made a by-word and scoffing? Walter! kneeling at his feet, he spurned me as he would have a dog. Is it not sufficient anguish to be thus driven from my husband? and to lose

you? for you are dying — O, my brother!
— I never harmed *you;* and I know in
your last hours you will not rashly do anything to increase *my* wretchedness!"

"You say truly, I cannot live; and the
good Priest has this day told me that only
by confession, can I hope myself to be forgiven.   I must *not* bear this secret with me
to the grave."

"Walter! have mercy upon me — upon
me — your sister; or I am lost, undone!"

"Dearest! even for you I cannot risk the
bliss of heaven.   Anita! meet me there!
As a "Sister of Charity," atone for the
past; and with the blessings of the unfortunate upon your head, enter Paradise!"

That day — the dearly beloved, *absolved*
brother closed his eyes in death.

That day — the heart-broken, despairing
Anita was placed in charge of Sister Irene.

And that day — Gustave received through

an unknown source, in the handwriting of
Walter, his friend at the last, a full confession of the wicked deception practiced upon
him by his sister — and by himself — the
dead!

CHAPTER XXIII.

THE LETTER.

" For a letter, timely writ, is a rivet to the chain of affection."

WHY could I not altogether have banished my late unhappy experience?

Why not — to the end — have remained independent and self-reliant?

It was not to be.

I was in the power of an irresistible·Destiny.

The Fates were busily weaving the dark web of my future; elaborating day by day the everlasting truth,

> " The mills of the gods grind slowly,
> But they grind exceeding small."

I suffered; more than I chose to acknowledge.

Was I never again to know peace?

Was every anticipated happiness to be-come ashes in my grasp?

I withdrew, as of old, into myself. I nursed in secret my grief. I no longer found anything in outward circumstance to give pleasure; and I discovered too late — that I had ventured my all upon the truth-fulness of one man — and had lost!

I knew, moreover, that man was wretched.

All could have been saved by the frank avowal of his secret marriage.

True — fear of losing — had been his ex-cuse for not informing me sooner.

Through this selfish motive he had blasted the prospects of both.

I could not forgive; him — for bringing upon me this new trouble; myself — for blindly trusting where I really knew so little.

Meanwhile, armed with his precious doc-ument Gustave proceeded at once to lay it before the proper authorities.

His previous statement being so well substantiated, he had now no difficulty in getting from the court his papers. To his infinite relief his marriage vow was disannulled, and he pronounced at liberty!

The " cursed knot " was at length untied.

But what course should he now pursue?

How convince her he loved, that his honor was unimpeached?

He wrote; and the same day that was telegraphed the all comprehensive word " FREE! " — I received this letter: —

" *Ma chere Amie,* — Blame me not. The devotion of my life shall prove to you I am not unworthy. *Ecoutez !* My situation was perplexing in the extreme. United in marriage by force — to as it were a stranger — never heeding for one moment her ardent protestations of undying affection; never seeing, in truth, her face from the hour of the illegal ceremony until I demanded my liberation; but utterly unable to prove all this; I have necessarily been under a cloud. Only the death of her brother saved me. During his sickness his burdened conscience gave him no rest; and at the last hour, regardless of the entreaties of his sister, he confessed to his Priest the whole; thus leaving it in my power, as an honorable man, to throw myself upon your forgiveness; and — may I hope? — upon your love. You are older than I. '*Qu'im-porte l'age?*' Do not, I beg, give one thought to the idle fancy *that* will ever affect my feelings towards you; for before my Maker, I declare to you — singular as it may appear — I never *have* loved but one, never *can* love but one, never shall *marry* but one. You, you alone, must henceforth prove my guiding star. *Adieu — Je pense toujours à vous, et mon cœur reste avec vous —* GUSTAVE."

This placed the entire matter in a new light.

I had now but to consider whether, against the judgment of my friends, I dared take the responsibility of marrying this man so many years my junior.

What does not love dare?

Ignoring all difference in age; in religion; in circumstance; in position: my life all passed; his all to come; and risking, as never before, my future upon this last throw — I again married!

CHAPTER XXIV.

THE HONEYMOON.

" Honey-sweet, but lacking not the bitter."

IMMEDIATELY upon our marriage we had secured a house in R—— Street and there collected our " household gods."

That was the happy era of my newly wedded life!

Gustave was devoted to me, and to all my interests; and worked hard to establish business plans upon a firm footing.

We were comfortably and pleasantly situated.

Our days glided peacefully on; our evenings made very enjoyable by books, music, and the society of friends.

I never tired of listening to his fine voice,

as, accompanied by the piano, he sang the ballads I loved.

In my contentment I surely refuted the " croak " that, in marrying Gustave, " I was rushing upon certain ruin ! "

And we were happy! We had a honey-moon!

No marriage — consummated though it be under the most disadvantageous, irre-concilable circumstances — but has *that.*

No two — *however* thrown together in the intimate relationship of man and wife — can fail to appreciate, and at first, find satisfac-tion in the new tie.

Novelty lends its powerful charm!

Both, too, are upon good behavior. All that is most agreeable and best in their " make up," is unconsciously displayed.

Annoying dissimilarities are not suffered to·appear.

Mutual " *politesse* " conceals these.

What a pity human nature is such uncer tain stuff that " familiarity breeds contempt;" and that knowing this — individuals, united for life, should ever allow this all important "*politesse*" to become a thing of the past!

The subject has been exhausted. Everything has been written and said to impress the fact that life is made up of trifles ; and that constant attention to these " trifles " is, most of all, essential to the newly married.

Burlesque has ridiculed the idea of a man devoting himself, and showing after marriage the attentions of the lover; but no burlesque, no ridicule can do away the " fixed fact," that upon these attentions depend all the happiness, and nearly all the affection, of the wife.

In this direction I had no cause for complaint.

My " Don Juan " had subsided into a most exemplary husband.

From the time of our meeting, his flirtation period had come to a sudden and complete " finis."

Still, he was not perfect.

His fiery nature had developed a suspicious, jealous disposition that the merest word excited.

True, he never raised his eyes to another — but what was not so satisfactory an accompaniment — he never permitted me to raise mine!

Necessarily, to avoid outbreaks, a good deal of valuable time was spent in the unprofitable exercise of " walking over eggs."

Taking all things into consideration, I have come to the settled conclusion that it is not desirable to be so exclusively an " object of interest."

Shadow of this *"grande passion "* — is Jealousy; which, as a bane to domestic peace, stands unrivaled!

There is no *reason* connected with it !

> " Trifles light as air,
> Are to the jealous, confirmation strong
> As proof of holy writ ! "

Per necessity; my friends, and many harmless pleasures went by the board.

All this was as nothing, however, in comparison with a danger that threatened to engulf my every comfort, my every hope, my every ambition.

Slowly, but surely it approached!

And after months of torturing suspense, the conviction was forced upon me, that undeniably well as my young husband loved me — he as undeniably loved his glass better.

CHAPTER XXV.

MY CREED.

"It is not for me to stipulate for creeds."

"By giving others many goods, to his own cost and hinderance."

I AM Orthodox!—always have been—through thick and thin!

I believe in the Lord.

He looketh from heaven upon the children of men ; and—in His high Omniscience—can determine to a dead certainty who among them needeth discipline.

He looked down. He saw me. He did not hesitate to put on the screws.

With Gustave, domestic life began slightly to pall.

Young men, the least bit fast—under

one pretense and another — were from time to time introduced into our circle, to give it a little more zest.

In spite of my remonstrance, they gradually obtained a hold upon my too yielding husband; and occasionally he accepted an invitation out.

Their influence began to tell. Business was neglected. His attentions to me assumed a little less of the lover-like.

About this time I lost heavily through the unforeseen, and as it affected me, dishonorable failure of parties with whom, during my widowhood, I had intrusted considerable property.

Misfortune with some, works just the reverse of what might be expected, or of what it ought!

So ours, instead of retarding the evil, but brought it the more surely and rapidly upon us.

Gustave became more than ever addicted

to the use of intoxicating drink ; and in his insane desire to drown trouble — attached himself to a set of associates — of the "most approved brand," to lead a genial, impulsive young man to his utter ruin.

"Josh Billings !"—thou *art* a Prophet! "if one commences to go down hill, everything *is* greased for that particular occasion!"

About this time, also, was initiated the one — I correct myself — the. two, great financial errors of my life.

"To raise the sinews of war," I placed myself in the power of a Loan Office; no — not a Loan Office — a Vampire; who sucked the very last drop of my heart's blood — with all the unconcern of a fox — contemplating his savory morsel — the bewildered chicken — he holds in his paws!"

"To raise the sinews of war," I placed myself in the power of friends; obtaining help here and there — hoped to stave off impending disaster — and in time, by aid of said help, retrieve all.

Delusive hope!

To-day, rather should Executors take every dollar ; the Sheriff every " household god ; " I — calmly gathering my garments, and emphasizing every note of

> " Shoo! Fly ; don't bother me " —

would walk into the most comfortable Poor House I could find — take the best room the law allowed — and,

> " Folding the drapery of my couch about me,
> Lie down to pleasant dreams."

CHAPTER XXVI.

BOSTON'S FEMALE BROKER.

"Until for surface sweetness, thou too art drawn adown the vortex."

PEOPLE said I was smart! I was: a little too smart: so I "pitched in" — to speculation!

I didn't walk in — nor run in — *I pitched in;* and came down head first, in which interesting position I have been ever since.

Permit me to explain.

Bewailing my losses, it flashed over me one day that by furnishing and sub-letting dwellings, I might do a pretty good thing.

Besides — I was anxious to become — a broker! *a female broker!!* BOSTON'S FEMALE BROKER!!!

With gain and ambition in view, I proceeded to hire a couple of houses at either end of a well known street; so that — whatever custom the one failed to get going up — the other could catch coming down.

I was fortunate in persons to run the same; and plumed myself no little on my sharp arrangements; was particular — that whatever leases I took should secure me from all loss; and was equally careful — in those I gave.

Of course I charged a stiff price; wasn't *that* the most important part of the business?

Making up my mind not to bother; not to see, in fact, my tenants; only as from time to time I collected my rent, I sailed off in rather an airy frame of mind.

All went well. I began to be encouraged.

From the house at the "upper end" I received my first month's pay.

That was square ; but I guess it took all the poor woman could rake and scrape ; for when I called at the end of the next month — she had gone

"Where the Woodbine twineth."

The house had changed hands three times ; and each lot had set up housekeeping on their "own hook," well supplied with my furniture, beds and bedding !

It then occurred to me, it would pay to look after furnished houses oftener than once a month.

"But I had still a "forlorn hope." The person at the "lower end ; " no sooner had she taken possession, however, than the furnace, which had faithfully done duty any number of years, gave out.

Generously, I immediately put a new one in its place at my own expense — privately thinking all the while — *my* landlord should foot that little bill.

I had reckoned without my host.

"Not for Joe ! O, no, no !"

nor for *me ;* and it took precisely the money I had received from the other house to set this one going!

So it went on. If those two houses had been sworn partners, they could not have played better into each other's hands.

" Paul paid Peter "; and " Peter paid Paul "; until there was nothing left to pay either " Peter " or " Paul "!

Distracted, I threw them both on to the market!

Napoleon, after his disasters, gathered himself and risked his final throw upon Waterloo.

The " Oakes Ames Co." suspended ; but with shovel in hand, have resumed their digging.

I too, was on my mettle!

It was still my determination to spec-ulate ; in Howard — not State Street. I have been told there is a difference ; do not confound them — *Howard* Street — if you please !

I outdid myself; and with unusual sa*
gacity selected a house completely out of
order from top to bottom.

We commenced this time at the top.

In dull times, set workmen to repair and
there is no knowing where they will end.
I have consulted competent judges, and
they tell me there is not a tighter roof in
all Boston.

An underpinning is considered desirable.
That was attended to.

The first person after the premises was
an Irishwoman, of the better class; who
was all ready to come right in with a large
family of boarders, about sixty I think;
hard-working men; who must have their
meals three times a day; at just such an
hour; to the minute.

The range would not go! I saw it myself; not a potato could be coaxed to bake,
not a sausage to fry; and right before
the face and eyes of those sixty hungry

wretches,.waiting for their dinner, the old thing was marched off, and a new stove set up!

Outside repairs, mine.   Inside, hers.

Poor soul! the expense came hard on her the first month; and as *she* didn't say anything about the rent, *I* couldn't find it in *my* heart to mention it.

I let it slip!

The second and third month it slipped!

I slipped, too!

But at the end of the fourth month, I had the satisfaction of slipping her — bag and baggage — stove and boarders — on to the sidewalk!

My investments were exciting, if not profitable.

The " real estate " business was getting red-hot!

I longed for the wilderness; for some far off, lone isle.

I would have married Robinson Crusoe on the spot.

No such relief was at hand; and walking right through the ingenious theories of Lucy Stone — Susan B. Anthony — and Antoinette Brown — I precipitately retired; not with "honors thick about me," but with dishonored notes so filling the air, I couldn't see my way home.

Never again shall the " Siren Song" of " Female Ability " induce *me* to run with my brother financier — as rival contestant for the prize — money.

No! Leaving him legitimately to make — I will agree, quite as fast, in the most lady-like manner — to spend it!

CHAPTER XXVII.

OLLA PODRIDA.

" Many thoughts, many thoughts — who can catch them all ? "

MATTERS now began to look dark indeed. Everything I touched went under. However much advice and acute judgment were brought·to bear, each investment fell through.

With the same implicit faith I put in the words of Mr. " Billings," do I believe GREASE — at that period — entered largely into *my* own composition; or I never could, in every case, have gone down so rapidly and — so *slick !*

A change became absolutely necessary. We could remain no longer in R—— Street. Debts increased every day; credit grew 'beautifully less "; Gustave's dissipated habits more confirmed. Friends turned the cold shoulder with the cheerful remark, "I TOLD YOU SO!" — and under these exhilarating circumstances — I made another move.

My Evil Genius, never for one moment caught napping, led me into N—— Street.

What could I do in N—— Street?

I looked around. My situation was desperate. I recalled with distrust the horrible old house in Howard Street; the furnished house in Harrison Avenue; the lodging-house in Washington Street; and concluded in N—— Street, by way of variety, to start a boarding-house.

I had been in New York — and came home determined to engraft the best qualities of *those* dashing institutions — upon the milder outcroppings of the same here.

Now you may advertise until the " Herald" retires, rich upon the profit of your investment, and not fill your house.   .

I just did this ; wrote in a fine, lady-like hand " Furnished Rooms to let "—"Table Boarders wanted "—and genteelly pasted the notice outside my door.

There is fashion in the width ; two inches there; four inches here. In reckless expenditure of paper, Boston goes New York double !

My table rapidly filled up.

It did me good to look upon that long line of thin forms, rounding each day at my expense.

Little did I think I was filling up a set of half-starved boarders — who, as soon as they got a streak of fat — would make for more aristocratic quarters.

It is one peculiarity of this business. All new boarding-houses go through the same ordeal. I have changed locality five times — and know!

Now — I am posted; the minute I clap my eyes on an "applicant," I can tell how much he will hold — to a biscuit !

I had partaken of so much HASH myself, that when I first commenced, I couldn't find it in my heart to offer it to a stranger.

I call upon you — O, my boarders! — first and last, seventy-five in number; from your scattered homes, answer me! Did I oftener than seven times a week set before you, in its decent proportions of meat and potato, that much abused dish?

Be genteel or die! I followed this to the letter; so of course — gentlemen — "only!"

Whoever heard of a *genteel* boarding-house harboring women?

Young ladies are "fuss and feathers;" and married ladies — well! — "Don't you think my dear there is a falling off in Miss Jones' table? — hadn't we better be looking out?"

Give me men! I say it boldly; you can impose upon *them;* you can't upon women!

How some boarders entwine themselves

11

around the affections! Parting, is like tak
ing your heart's blood; and leaving behind
them a blank, they go; bearing that most
sacred of trusts, an unpaid board bill; with
butter at fifty cents the pound!

Mine have "entwined," often.   Here is a
case in point.   .   .

I once lodged and fed a party of "Pro-
fessionals."   It seems but as yesterday.
Didn't they make times lively? Their
names are engraven on my heart — and on
my slate — for three left, owing me thirty-
six dollars!

The fourth! Let me do *him* exact justice.

From the fashionable time in the morning — when, alone, he ate his aristocratic
breakfast of one egg and a slice of toast —
all through the day; up to the hour of hiding his handsome face under a "mask of
color;" and with his witticisms throwing the
"house" into convulsions; he was a perfect
gentleman.

Pleasant to all; prompt to pay; a very small eater; he was indeed a model boarder. But — by that eternal law of compensation following a landlady the world over — the man who sat next him, ate his weight three times a day!

I have hinted that my *domestic* education had been somewhat neglected.

Still, I knew a thing or two — and what I *did* know — I never intrusted to others.

It became necessary to transfer the feathers from an old bed, to a new.

Waiting for a rainy day, that I might be secure from the interruption of calls, I shut myself up in a small room with my two ticks.

Mother had told me it was a good plan to leave part of each open — and inserting one into the other — gently force the feathers from the old to the new.

I was not to be trammeled with any such half-way idea!

I ripped open one entire end, and boldly emptied the feathers.

Whew! I was in for it!

Nothing daunted, with both hands I went to work. The day passed on. The job was finished. But myself!—

From the crown of my head to the sole of my foot —*feathers !*

Eyes, nose, mouth, ears, hair, eyebrows —*feathers !*

Like Nebuchadnezzar, I emerged: thankful for the next three months — to go to grass!

Gentility said, *colored* help! I submitted. My prime minister, Samuel Adams, was as black as the Ace of Spades.

Like all prime ministers, he ruled. I was a mere puppet — useful on Saturday nights — to "pay off."

He would notify me when he intended to go out "perzactly;" but failed to "put in an appearance" when expected home.

"One night he took his girl and his clothes to a concert." — Page 165.

He was musical — no matter what was up — negro melodies came "in at the death!"

He had a girl — more than that — he had a new suit of clothes. One night he took his girl and his clothes to a concert. Light pants and vest; dark coat, to match his skin; sleeve-buttons, he sent for me to put them in; and may I never see a rose-bud, if he didn't have one in his button-hole!

During his engagement at the Howard Athenæum I boarded Pfau, the Russian gymnast.

It was Sam's ambition to rival him.

Awakened one morning by a shuffling sound, I stole softly down. He had ar-ranged his apparatus — consisting of a rope swung in the wood-shed — and I caught him in the very act of making his fearful leap, from the top stair of the back steps to the hen-coop!

If he had missed his footing, he would have fallen just three feet, four inches.

In the matter of food he was fastidious. Eggs he couldn't bear the sight of,— I had nine hens and one rooster — and I never saw an egg while Sam was in the house!

But the milk! *that* corn he acknowledged; and if he-couldn't go out as *wet nurse*, it *was not* because he had NO MILK!

One colored brother will do, but five! My kitchen was the " blackness of darkness." I couldn't see through it!

The next experiment was not much more satisfactory. All white, to be sure; that was something in the way of looks! I felt too, that somehow the dinner would come on to the table; but at what a sacrifice of the " raw material." And " back-door friends " was a disagreeable feature — necessitating the appointment of a " Vigilance Committee " — if the saving of cold victuals was any object.

But trying to mingle the Hibernian and African in the way of help — I am free to confess — was the most unmitigated failure of all.

They were set like a flint against each other. In attempting to elicit one spark of united assistance, I only set fire to myself.

"Gentlemen! I put the question!" Can the mistress of a boarding-house know anything outside her kitchen? Above all — can she be expected to improve her mind? to read? — dear me! one eye on the sugar and the other on the spoons, where's her chance?

Descending from the *literary* stand-point, I suppose there is no gainsaying that some houses, in spite the hindrances, do succeed; and the landladies thereof — rising, Phœnix-like, above the perplexity of help; the inconvenience of loss; smiling and popular — wear pink ribbons!

CHAPTER XXVIII.

PANDEMONIUM.

" How have I sinned that this affliction
Should light so heavy on me ? "

"In the scene that ensued
I did not take a hand. "

I HAD discovered *pink* was not my color
I always wore black; and in mourning
would prefer to drop the curtain; leave to
imagination the " after-piece; " but inex-
orable Truth compels me to go on.

Our house was large ; the expense of furnishing had been heavy. The locality too,
was unfortunate; still, at 'first, as I have
said, there appeared to be no difficulty in
getting boarders, hungry table boarders;
and I flatter myself that alone, I could have
made this last experiment pay.

But alone, I was not suffered to engineer.

A candle, about to expire, flares up with unexpected brilliancy.

Curiously enough this original metaphor, coupled with the equally original " saw ; " " What is sauce for a goose, is sauce for a gander ; " will admirably apply to me, the goose ; and to Gustave, the gander.

I was about to expire financially — (pity I hadn't sooner !) — and collected myself for a last flicker.

Gustave was about to wind up his dissipated term, and gathered his forces for a last " free blow."

To that end — he established a BAR ! — though I went down on my knees to beg off from *that.*

I found it took ready money to get in a stock of liquors.

Dealers in the infernal stuff know their power ; and whatever other bills are dishon ored ; theirs are paid at sight.

Their books, to the interest of their ple
thoric pockets, present accounts well posted
and paid up.

Smarting under this fact, I am happy in
the thought, that one day there will be
thrust before their astonished eyes a private memoranda, that will require all their
wits to settle ; though assisted by Satan him
self — head bookkeeper — LOCATED THERE !

The bar went on — ignored by the better
class of my boarders — who soon ignored
the house, also.

But many, young and inexperienced, attracted by the cheerful, well-lighted room,
found their way thither; and far into the
night the rattling of dice, and the uncork-
ing of bottles, fell upon my listening ear.

Did I say *Jealousy*, as a bane to domestic
peace, stands unrivaled ?

I retract !

My views are liberal.   I believe in good

hard-shell Baptists; and in good Hottentots, I believe good may result from the awful crime of murder ; and that good may come of the African slave-trade.

But, accursed liquor! in *thee* there is no good. Emanating from hell — through and through, from top to bottom — thou art one, unmitigated Evil!

By love of thee ; the most gifted — become driveling. The most genial — morose. The most loving — demoniac.

To unhallowed thirst for thee ; accursed liquor! God, wife, children, friends, home, clothes, food, self-respect and life, all are sacrificed ; and underneath the ceaseless roll of thy wheels, O, thrice accursed liquor! more are crushed than ever fell before the triumphal car of the Indian Juggernaut!

Why, upon me and mine, had descended the fell destroyer?

From infancy, I had abominated this foul outcropping of total depravity.

My·father before me, had lost thousands because of not offering, at a dinner party on board his ship, the hateful thing, to a person . addicted to its use, who never forgave the slight !

But come it did, with all its 'attendant train of degrading humiliations.

To the theatrical profession I am indebted for many pleasant hours.

I am an extravagant admirer of the " Legitimate Drama ; " and in my palmy days was a liberal patron of the same.

But geologically speaking there is a lower strata ; and *that* found its way to Gustave's " free blow." ˚

It must have been a *hungry* strata ; for each day, to the music of the bell, a string of those Bohemians formed themselves in order of march from the " bar " to my dinner‐table ; led off by that prince of dead‐heads — Monsieur Antoine Tournais — who had managed to fasten himself upon Gustave with all the tenacity of a drowning man.

"*Entre nous,*" it is my private opinion he would have been drowned long ago, only he was so thoroughly soaked with brandy, there was no room for water!

In return for Gustave's hospitality, he volunteered to distribute some advertising bills.

I do not know whether he had a shirt to his back, but I *do* know he had a pair of white gloves; with which, and his eternal "*pardonnez madame,*" he electrified the female help who answered, as he went from door to door, his aristocratic ring.

I certainly consider that man, with his slippers and white stockings, and a monkey, borrowed a few days to lend additional style, at once the disgrace and ornament of this MODEL *bar!*

"*Requiescat in pace.*" I hope his friends have found a use for that epitaph, and that — poor fellow — he is indeed at rest.

I am now speaking of Monsieur Antoine Tournais, not of his friend, the monkey!

All housekeepers know that cooks like a cup of that which " cheers, but not inebriates ; " and like it strong too!

My cooks reversed Cowper's apologetic idea; and absolutely required a cup of that which, however much it " inebriated " them, failed to " cheer " me.

We had dinner, as Sam said, " perzactly " at twelve o'clock.

One day, during the black and white episode, about half-past eleven, my pastry cook — white — took herself and her inebriating facilities bodily out of the house ; and I have not laid eyes on her since ; when she knew that my meat cook — black — was up in her attic on a three days' drunk!

> " But the hands that were played
> By that heathen Chinee,
> And the points that were made
> Were quite frightful to see."

The wind is tempered to the shorn lamb — or the shorn lamb is tempered to the wind — as I am not quoting Scripture, I forget which.

N'importe.

There never was a shorn lamb born, that could walk up to the wind I had to face ' and there never was a wind blew, that my temperature was not put to its test !

CHAPTER XXIX.

INFERNO.

"And so he drinks the more and damns himself —
Then drinks again, and sleeps and wakes and raves."

"Woe is me, that I sojourn in Mesech,
That I dwell in the tents of Kedar!"

A RUSH from the bed to the door — and "Sam!" uttered in stentorian voice — rings through the house!

Sam appears; goes to the chimney-piece; takes therefrom an empty bottle; disappears; and returns it filled to the same place.

This scene has been repeated many times, every day, for one week. If I told the truth, I should say three.

Gustave, not to mince the matter, is on a drunk.

Will he ever be on anything else?

I have misused the word. You cannot get him drunk.

He is on a drink; and he will challenge you to that, until *you* drop.

The pure juice of the grape, I have no doubt, is a very delectable article.

When freely used, even in remote ages, it no further "set up" Noah; than to make him father the sons of Ham! No further "set up" the rather an-eye-to-the-main-chance, young man, Lot; than to bring out his harmless joke, that his old, salt wife had no objection to his taking to his bosom a young, fresh one! No further "set up" Abraham's wife, Sarai; than to make her tell two outrageous lies; and beat Hagar almost to death into the bargain!

The pure juice of the grape nowadays, is grown in hell; and whosoever imbibes the brimstone mixture there pressed, goes

12

through a series of antics initiated in that hot clime.   •

Thus, with Gustave.

To this day I am in doubt, and cannot pronounce, whether I prefer the phase of the driveling, tear-shedding, maudlin, hard drinker; or the free-fight, knock-down-and-drag-out development!

I ought to be a judge.   My brother was the one; my husband the other.

With the first, my life was safe; but the experience — sickeningly enervating.

With the last, my life was in danger; but the experience — inspiringly exciting.

Upon the cat-love-the-mouse principle, Gustave always insisted having me in sight when a " spree " was on him; and his " insist," I could not dodge.

After drinking, tossing, and tumbling; tumbling, tossing, and drinking, until apparently exhausted; he had fallen into an uneasy, fitful slumber.

All was quiet.

By and by he slightly stirred. Pitying, I approached to bathe his head; and softly laid my cool hand upon his burning fore-head.

Quicker than thought he dashed it from him.

"Away with your ——— hand! Never you dare, vile woman, to touch me again!"

"But, Gustave! it is me, your wife."

"———! you are no wife of mine. Go finish your talk with Mr. F——. You can't deceive *me*, try your best; what I see, I know. My eye is upon you — my fine bird — and *this* time you won't escape!"

"Gustave! I have not spoken one word to Mr. F—— for" —

"Go to ——! I wouldn't take your Bible oath that you haven't made arrangements to go off together. You man seducer. Don't you attempt to fool me; but if it costs me my life, I'll cut short your little game!"

I saw what was coming, in the jealous frenzy to which he had now wrought himself, and sprang for the door.

He was there before me. He had locked it; and holding the key at arm's length, brandished it triumphantly over my head.

How handsome he was in his mad wrath!

So looked " Lucifer," " Son of the Morning; " when, fallen, he announced in solemn conclave, his choice to

" Reign in Hell, than serve in Heaven."

"You thought you would go for your lover, did you? Perhaps you will, when I am dead; but that won't be till I've finished you. I'll not leave *you*, with your paramour, to gloat over *my* ruin. If it hadn't been for you, devilish deceiver! I should never have drank a drop. You have driven me to it; and now I'll pour down the cursed stuff till I'm mad, ha! ha!"

"And dragging me before the mirror." — Page 181.

" Gustave ! Gustave ! in mercy to your self " —

" Don't ' Gustave ' me ! To *you*, Madame, I am Monsieur Chaudet. Running away from me, were you ? that won't pay; look here! my beauty! "

And dragging me before the mirror; that I might see, as well as feel ; he pressed both hands tightly over my mouth and nose.

I could not breathe. I was suffocating. I gave one despairing glance ; my face was purple; my eyes were starting from their sockets ——

God in Heaven! mine hour had come !

Swifter than the passage of light the prayer, " FORSAKE ME NOT," went up, with the faith of the dying, into the very ear of the Omnipresent; and brought down in-stant relief.

The hands relaxed their hold — and I was again numbered with the living !

" Gustave ! Gustave ! you would kill me with your own hand ! "

" Kill *you*, my darling, precious wife! I'd like to find myself — or any other person — laying the weight of their finger upon you."

Was the man in his senses?

Didn't he know that Murder had almost branded his soul?

" Gustave! dear Gustave! I implore you to lie down. You need rest. Let me open the door? I must go out from here, indeed I must! "

" Indeed you mustn't; and by Heaven! you won't. Going after your Mr. F——, were you? —— and ——! The handsomest man in State Street, eh!—. ' How is that for high?' *My* memory is good "—

" O, Gustave! give me that key? "

" —— you! sit down in that chair; and if you value your life, don't move."

" O! but I am nearly dead. I MUST have air;"—and mortal fright overcoming my dread of him, I shrieked for "help! help!"

" Didn't I tell you not to move ? ———
your soul to — ! take that " — and a BLOW,
heavy and unerring, descended upon my
devoted head.

White, as the sheeted dead, I faced my
foe.

Thus far, only *Fear* had influenced me;
but now, every passion was let loose.

Sorrow, Pity, Love, Hatred; and high
over all *revenge;* a burning thirst for RE-
VENGE, upon the infatuated, lost Gustave.

Had my strength equaled my will, the
powdered dust of his " mother earth " would
never have recognized her own !

Had I held the thunderbolts of Jove !

A man, younger than myself !

A man, for whom I had sacrificed so
much !

A man, to strike *me*, a woman !

Me, his wife !

Me, in whose veins coursed the blood of
five hundred aristocrats ! but every drop of
which was now like molten lead.

My whole being was in arms!

Single-handed I could have fought Satan.

I had not only Satan, but for the time being, his prime minister, Gustave.

It was two to one!

Benumbed alike, with the blow upon my head; and with the blow upon my heart; living — I sank to the floor — as one that was dead.

CHAPTER XXX.

THE HEGIRA.

"So I saw despondency was death, and flung my burdens from me."

"They were so queer, so very queer,
I laughed as I would die."

MEANTIME —

"'Midst the wreck of matter, and the crush of worlds" —

I held on to my reason. Poor me! It was about all I had to hold on *to;* except — my Saratoga trunk!

That I packed; and one Sunday, secretly left in the evening train for New York; leaving my planet, "without let or hindrance," to roll on, or go to smash, amid her sister spheres.

It is the evening of the day I arrived; bright and cool.

I really feel the need of recreation; and putting aside " Cooper Institute " facilities — " Shakespearian Readings "— " Operatic Librettos "— I am going to the Circus: the New York, Fourteenth Street, Circus.

I want to hear " Williams" sing; see " Stickney " ride; exercise my mind over " Billy Button;" as he tumbles into the ring; scrabbles on to his horse; throws off coats — vests — pants — boots — and appears before my dilating eyes — a first-class rider — radiant in scarlet and gold !

I am on my way ! Want to know how I look? dark green, poplin dress; black velvet sack; with one geranium leaf— one tuberose — one verbena — stuck in the button-hole.

That bouquet is stereotyped. No one ever saw me at the Fourteenth Street Circus without it.

I anticipate the cheerful salutation and exclaim, " We are all here; hope *you* are well, Mr. Clown ! "

The Band strikes up. I am ears and eyes.

Here they come; in the systematic con-fusion of the " *Grand Entrée.*"

Gallant men; fair women; gayly capar-isoned horses; true to your paces in the mazy intricacies of the sprightly waltz.

The "glamour" over, I pick my Knight.

Pale face — fair hair — slight, muscular figure — long limbs — (he will use all their length by and by in his famous " Four in Hand ;") showing beneath the Andalusian mantle an occasional glimpse of his colors — blue and fawn; and his horse? — light — but " with very little of the Arabian — my dear sir!" — give you his picture.

What have we here? " Plantation Bit-ters," with two crosses — XX — kicked about in this shape? regardless of cost ; and always upwards? — never a fall; give the law of gravitation a chance, and send these Bitters after it. O, the barrels are empty?

all right! — go ahead! — but do Mr. " Lev-
antine " make *one* mistake ; or I shall think
you hail from " Tartarus ; " and for morning pastime have taken a foot practice with
" Beelzebub ! "

" Whoa, January ! " — *Will* that man and
his establishment be the death of me ?
Shall I have a chance at another meal ?

If I was a boy ! — if I was a darkey ! if I
was only *anything*, that could spread right
out, and scream !

" Whoa, January ! " you *are* " Whoad "
with a vengeance ; and to start either wagon, nag, or driver, is beyond all save the
Pony, that opportunely comes to the rescue, and backs the precious *trio* out of sight.

The music changes. ——

Here you are my little lady ! with your
brief, gossamer skirts.

That is right; make your courtesy to the
expectant crowd.

I kiss you my hand !

The "ring master" awaits your dainty foot. Spring lightly to your saddle; not that — "as to the manor born" — spring lightly to the *bare back* of your impatient steed.

Away! white robe — pink shoulder knots — trailing flowers — in the rapid whirl — are but as the changes of a Kaleidoscope.

Away! right *through* the twelve hoops, placed to stay your flight.

Bravo! you have well won the tumultuous applause.

Bravo! again. With thoughts intent upon that "Aërial Feat" — there is no one I should so* like to be *this* night — as " Madame Caro*lène* Roland ! "

Hurra! for the " Blue and Fawn; " as — with the rush of the wind — " Stickney's " " Four in Hand " sweeps past; guided by his masterly skill.

From my distant seat *I* catch his " *allez* ! " hissed between his teeth; and instantly rec-

ognizing the voice his coursers quicken —
if possible — their already lightning speed.

Now, gathering his reins — the panting
'four" are side by side — and over all
hovers the graceful form of the daring
rider !

Now, throwing up his reins — and lightly
balancing himself upon one foot on the
" leader " — the loosened " four " dash
wildly around the arena.

> " One stormy gust of long suspended ahs !
> One whirlwind chaos of insane hurras ! "

But *"au revoir."* I will put my " verbena " — my " tuberose " — my " geranium
leaf" into water — and come again to-morrow night.

Being somewhat acquainted, I had gone
directly to the hospitable house of a quondam landlady.

I found her neatly arrayed in a brown
silk ; narrow pink ribbons floating from her

stylish head-dress; and a rich, pink bow, of most approved dimensions, at her throat.

Noticing my mourning, but relieved to learn that none of my immediate friends were dead, she entered into friendly talk; and suggested, for our mutual enjoyment, several little excursions.

Remember! I had two distinct natures; and that "fair play is a jewel."

The gloomy and sad had been indulged long enough; if I expected to preserve the balance of power — or more truthfully speaking — the balance of reason; so I fell in with her plans.

With my dressy friend — and the joyous half · of my "*personelle*" — I had, for the next ten days, a right down good time.

I would not think of home — positive "Nemesis" would be on my track only too soon — and my flight avenged!

We often rode round "Central Park" — twenty-five cents apiece for the whole distance — thanks to the new arrangement.

We often sailed down to " Staten Island " — ten cents each way — and in this rational, economical mode, passed many a happy day.

> " On old Long Island's sea-girt shore,
>   Many an hour I've whiled away;
> Listening to the breakers' roar,
>   That wash the beach at Rockaway."

There came a telegram.   They were sick. *Who* was sick, I wondered ?

That afternoon, in the most unconcerned manner, I took another turn at " Central Park."

There came a second telegram.   They were very sick.

Who was very sick, I wondered ?

That day I steamed down to " Staten Island," in a perfectly tranquil state of mind.

When I had " touched bottom " — it occupied me longer than it did " Gail Hamilton " (for my own convenience), I turned my face homewards.

The BAR had disappeared. Carpet and furniture had converted it into a comfort-able-sitting room.

The two large parlors made one grand dining-room ; where waiters by the score, flying round like mad, were serving custom-ers at forty cents a head !

Without an allusion to the past, I was humbly requested, as Cashier, to step into that exciting establishment — known in Boston — as the " Narragansett House."

13

CHAPTER XXXI.

THE GRAND FINALE.

"I cannot add — I will not steal; enough, for all is spoken."
"For the things
Concerning me have an end."

IT was Gustave who was sick. It was Gustave who was very sick; of his liquor — of his *bar* — of HIMSELF!

I trace the incipient, embryo purpose of reformation to my strategetic " Hegira."

My influence again somewhat reinstated, I set myself steadily to reform many abuses; dismissed a gang of " Cormorants " in the shape of " hangers on " and " help ; " retrenched in every way ; looked right sharp after affairs ; and if Gustave had even now taken a complete turn round, we might, after all our mishaps, have in a measure saved ourselves.

But he was a boon companion, and could not be spared from his set.

He was generous; and fell into the too common error of being so at other peoples' expense; so that, the little I had left — dwindled to less; and it became evident everything must go.

I will be just to him, though I implicate myself.

If from the first I had been more decided — held to my " rights " — a good deal of subsequent "unpleasantness" might have been avoided; but I was naturally confiding, and hard experience alone, will remove that weakness.

He who begins by trusting everybody, ends by trusting none!

If ever, in the flesh, I do get hold of a cent — well! — " *nous verrons.*"

I was now in the condition of " Micawber," waiting for " something to turn up."

Unlike that renowned man, I was not disappointed.

Something did "turn up" —

A KEEPER was put in; with strict orders not to leave the premises without the money in his pocket!

"Yea, mine own familiar friend, in whom I trusted, which did eat of my bread, hath lifted up his heel against me." — *Psalms* xli. 9.

For the benefit of those who have never had such companionship foisted upon them — let me state; that the security of a respectable Toad, under a harrow, is Elysian compared with it.

Lynx-eyed, sitting where he could command "the situation," not one thing escaped his notice.

I drank my very tea in fear and trembling, lest there should be a "slip between the cup and my lip."

Miraculously disposing of that "Incubus," I rushed to our principal creditor, and begged him, for the love of Heaven, to come down and put such an attachment on the place, as would wind up that, myself, and everybody concerned.

This he did; and in an inconceivably short space of time — considering the number of articles to be touched by the magic wand of going! *going!* GONE! — everything I owned in the world, for the second time, under the hammer of a voluble auctioneer, was knocked down to the highest bidder!

I actually felt relieved.

I had reached the last round of the ladder; but one more step and I should kiss my " mother earth."

That spectacle was in reserve.

Not being " woman's rights," I never made a public speech.

Going back eighteen months, I wish I could assemble every individual I owe in this wide world, and say unto them —

"Gentlemen!— I am a woman; and as such, have the meanest possible opinion of my capacity to transact business.

"My mother erred; in that, she did not learn me to cook.

> "'The devil finds some mischief still
> For idle hands to do.'

"If I had been a good cook, I should not have been a poor financier.

"You are the victims of her unfortunate mistake.

"I owe you collectively a good deal of money.   I have not one cent wherewith to repay.

"I throw myself upon your mercy.

"I am going to New York to hide my humiliating defeat — and am indebted to the kindness of a friend — for a free pass thereto.   Farewell."

CHAPTER XXXII.

RESURGAM.

" And all in sympathy with thee, tremble with tumultuous emotions."

THE broken-down of all nations congregate in New York.

To that conglomerate centre I accordingly wended my ardent steps.

I had now my " free pass " — and my clothes.

The " pass " was taken up in my transit. My clothes I expected to meet on my arrival.

They were not there!

I had sent them on in care of Gustave, who had preceded me. He had gone into business, and had raised his share of the partnership money — upon them!

The last round in the ladder slipped out ; my feet flew up ; I came down flat on my back.

I HAD NOTHING —

Quite agreed with " Dick Swiveller " that an umbrella would be something ; but my umbrella was invested in — a Bleecker Street restaurant!

Poor Gustave! He had hoped through successful custom to make good my loss, before I discovered it.

But the old, uncontrollable habit got the upper hand. His business, as usual, proved a failure ; and my best clothes still grace the shelves of a Prince Street pawnbroker!

CHAPTER XXXIII.

" Which I wish to remark —
　　And my language is plain —
　　That for ways that are dark
　　And for tricks that are vain,
　　The heathen Chinee is peculiar.
　　Which the same I would rise to explain."

THE account of Dr. Kane's explorations
in the ice-bound region of the North is interesting ; because — it is true.

The account of Dr. Livingstone's travels
in the burning region of the South is interesting ; because — it is true.

This chapter will be interesting; because
— it is true.

I had three choice articles of wearing ap-
parel left,

I was hungry. They must go to sat‑
isfy that hunger; and after shedding tears
enough over each separate piece to start a
reasonable Niobe in a fair business, I set
out.

What was the use of dodging so many
corners? wearing myself to death trying to
deceive people?

My landlady knew everything in that bun‑
dle just as well as I did. How suspiciously
she eyed me as I passed out ; for all I took
such good care to keep my plump figure
between IT and her.

And the policeman on the corner; didn't
he know just as well as I — who tied up the
things — that within the thick paper, so
carefully done up, was my muff? — O! how
I have needed it this cold winter; my warm
beaver sack? — and my pretty, point-lace
collar? — that I never looked at without
recalling the black eyes of the coquettish
girl who sold it me in Montreal!

" Forewarned, forearmed." I had an idea that " Cops " could see right through a mill-stone ; so was mighty careful to trip by *him* airy and indifferent, specially to the package dangling by its strong string from my finger.

I didn't stop to ask the way to Canal Street. No. I crossed over to a good look-ing darkey — sunning himself and a cheap cigar on the sidewalk — and inquired.

What was the matter ? didn't anybody ever before carry a thick, brown, paper par-cel through Canal Street?

The fellow had one of his African eyes on it all the time he was pointing out the way!

I'm near-sighted; where am I ? O ! here it is; the very place. Underground shop; yes — door, part wood ; top, glass ; all the panes excepting one, painted white to screen the customers ; and that shows up in black letters, " Money to Loan ! — on Diamonds — Watches — Pianos."

But I have not got any " Pianos — Watches
—Diamonds : " what to do ? I stand irresolute.

A small, sharp-eyed man spied me, and
hurrying up said, " What can we do for you
marm, this morning ? " — all the while taking in the dimensions of my budget; and
I will wager my sapphire ring, now in the
hands of Mr. A—— as security, that he
knew exactly what was inside, and had
already made up his mind precisely how
much to advance on the lot!

Hiding my confusion, I gave elaborate
reasons for troubling so courteous a gentleman as himself, with the trifling affair. But,
with many apologies, " the fact was — I
wished to surprise a friend with a gift — and
being just a little short of funds — and
having read his advertisement in the " Herald " — I had taken the liberty to bring with
me a few things; which, if he would be so
obliging as to examine — and could be so

"What can we do for you, marm, this morning?" — Page 204.

kind as to give me some money upon — I should esteem it a very great favor — and would throw all the custom in his way I possibly could — ever after."

" O ! with pleasure, marm." Should he look at them ?

I wonder the " things " were not turned into salt by the abominable lie I had manufactured ; for, if he *hadn't* taken them, my " friend " would not have lost a gift, but I should have gone supperless to bed ; which, as I had not yet seen my dinner, " *n'y pensons pas !*"

" And what, marm, may you want on this collar ? "

"Well ! it cost me fifteen dollars ; but I don't suppose you will allow more than half that ! "

" Expect — me — to — allow — seven — dollars — fifty — cents — on — THAT ! " exclaimed the Jew, holding up the strip of lace two inches wide, fourteen inches long.

"One dollar twenty-five cents is the very most ; and we do that to accommodate *you*, marm ! "

I thought of my muff—my sable muff ; my sack — my beaver sack ; and groaned in spirit.

The man caught the echo of the groan ; looked into my face ; and " set on edge " with desire to make money, determined to drive a bargain.

All I could get out of him for the muff, which cost me twenty dollars, was a paltry two ; all for the sack, which cost me forty dollars, was a paltry four ; and both nearly new.

But I was the gainer in one way. I had no " transparency " to carry through the street; and I went up Broadway, with seven dollars twenty-five cents in my pocket, as lightly as though I had not got to pay, for the use of that bewildering amount, at the end of one short month, fourteen dollars and fifty cents ; besides running the risk of never getting back into my possession the aforesaid " articles."

I went home. I had my supper; and impulsively generous, invited Jane Matthews to sup with me.

We enjoyed it. Muffs, sacks, collars *do* eat well; and we had coffee, too. *That* upon my weak stomach, rather " set me up."

We played a two-handed game of Euchre in which, imitating that " heathen Chinee," I made some " points; " naturally enough, having just swallowed my point-lace collar !

At ten we separated. At eleven I went to bed; or rather threw myself on the sofa until my husband should come in.

I slept. Attend to my dream —

A good-sized dining-room ; carpet green and red; showing up bright in the full blaze of the gas. Gustave always would turn on that, regardless of the monthly call of the Manhattan Gas Light Co. The table set out — O! so nice — with its new dishes; and — I thought I saw a white cloth? no — I thought I saw a great sheet of white paper? no — it is the " New York Herald," all covered over with " Money to Loan ! " " Money to Loan ! " in letters a yard long.

But the fragrant odor of a well-cooked dinner comes stealing in at the open door; through which too, enters my husband. I am *so* glad.

The waiter sets down a large tureen right over the word " Money," leaving only " to Loan " bristling all around.

Is the *money* gone, and nothing left but the LOAN ?

I writhe in my sleep !

For the oysters. Gustave lifts the cover; and poking about the dish, angrily screams to the cook, " What is this mess ? "

" Just what mistress ordered, sir ! — seasoned it the best I knew how, sir ! — she would have muff for dinner, with oyster sauce."

"Yes — Gustave! my muff; they fare worse in Paris; eat away. It will digest quicker and much easier than my piano; that was rosewood; and you are used to logwood, you know! Pass me the end of that tassel, please, with a good deal of the gravy! Have some coffee?"

"Yes — milk it well; I will sugar myself. *Are* you crazy? Here's half your collar in the bottom of my cup, and the other half in my throat. Who told you, Bridget, to settle your coffee with lace collars?"

"Nobody, sir! mistress said fry it for breakfast; but as I looked at you, coming up the steps, sir, I thought may be, you would like it better *soaked.*".

"You and your mistress go to hell! The next thing, we shall have her sack served up for dinner."

"To-morrow, sir! Got it roasting now; it

14

is awful tough; won't be done clear through before your next meal. What kind of vegetables? — whiskey, or point-lace? — Sir!"

"*My* whiskey is point-lace, muff, beaver sack; but it is not for *you* to fling it at me; take that — you officious fool!" bawled Gustave; hurling tureen, muff, and all, after the flying cook. ·

I awoke with a start —

There was the green and red carpet, with the gas turned on to its full extent.

There sat Gustave with those three pawn tickets, that had fallen from my pocket, in one hand; and a boot, he had just pulled off to send after the first, in the other.

Tears were in his eyes. Conscience was at work.

I thought it no more than fair it should work, though the leaven of it rose him high as "Haman's gallows;" as — but for his impoverishing dissipation — I should now have round me, my widely scattered com forts.

My dream shadowed the truth.

The demon, Drink, pollutes everything it touches!

The demon, Drink, destroys everything that crosses its path!

The demon, Drink, inaugurates a series of " dissolving views " startling to the generally accepted, cohesive habits of " household gods ! "

While it is a law of Nature, that the less shall precede the greater; it is a law of this Monster, that the "greater" shall precede the "less."

The grand piano, that once occupied the whole side of a handsome room, has dwindled to a printed slip, my finger can cover, labeled — " Loan Ticket No. 1009 " — somewhat retrieving its *in*significance, in size; by its *si*gnificance, in import.

Verily, the Greater *hath* preceded the Less; substituting Discord for Harmony, in its unnatural priority!

Tokens, endeared by associations and years of possession, are gobbled up by " The Insatiable ; " that spews out of his foul mouth in return, strips of yellow paper, all looking one way.

Bah! I could paste " Tammany Hall ' from floor to ceiling, with the hateful color!

CHAPTER XXXIV.

BOOK AGENTS WANTED.

"By cheerful wit and graphic tale, refreshing the harassed spirit."

" Vive ! " New York! Down with Brooklyn !

This has not always been my war-cry. Time was, I sympathized with the " City of Churches."

But, let me tell. —

The boarding-house, and every other scheme, having signally failed, thereby sinking my entire means; nothing less than starvation, staring me directly in the face, could have induced my next step.

Pitying Shade! Guardian Angel! wast thou asleep, when I answered the above " want ? "

To break myself in, make myself "*au fait*" to the business; I selected Brooklyn as the place; and a mongrel affair, half receipts — half advertisements — as the base of, operation.

Already I emulated the maid of "green gown" memory; and my eggs had bought, only she knew, how much.

Brooklyn was to hatch the chickens!

So, decked in borrowed plumage, a black lace shawl carelessly thrown over me for effect, hopes high, anticipations brilliant, to Brooklyn I went!

To be explicit —

My commission upon each number sold was to be ten cents.

"*En passant,*" the publisher had secured the lion's share, and had taken his pay in advance.

Behold me! a novice! and raw at that; with twenty-five pamphlets that had fallen dead from the press, as my only capital, save — my tongue.

I used that freely; and did more talking over those money-saving receipts, and self-sacrificing advertisements, than would have set up the entire New York Bar, in a first-class practice!

Either, all "heads of families" in Brooklyn were "petrified," "*à la* Cardiff giant;' or, servants had received strict orders to admit no vagrants.

Only two American faces greeted my vision that blessed day.

However, perseverance wins; and by dint of my sweetest smiles; my extremest politeness; my shawl poetically arranged; I did sell, through the agency of these same servants, *six* of my precious load.

Sixty cents clear gain. Fifteen cents to be deducted for car fare.

I indulged in no dinner; made *that* out of my New York landlady at night.

For three days, I continued thus. The miles of streets I walked; the acres of steps

I ascended : then — following the example of the

"King of France, with forty thousand men " —

descended; are they not forever memorialized in my failing limbs ?

Brooklyn! adieu! I shake thy dust off my feet!

From thy sympathetic, Ferry-begirt area, I bore an exact profit of one dollar and twenty-eight cents; and — an experience.

But, turning, the El Dorado of the "agent" meets my longing gaze.

Dirty! Noisy! Splendid! — New York! I salute you!

No more worthless pamphlets. A genuine book, could alone satisfy my aspirations.

What should it be ?

Up and down the columns of the "New York Herald" mine eyes roved in eager search.

" Book Agents wanted!" met me at every turn.

At length I hit upon just the thing. Volume nice'; author well known ; profit good.

With unquestioning faith, I entered the arena as "agent " for *that* work.

Recalling the past, I eschewed dwellings. Most women prefer ribbon to literature, when it comes to actually paying for the same.

I looked solely to places where men " most do congregate," for patronage.

Pride, sensitiveness and — yes — delicacy too, must go by the board, if success is the goal, in this calling.

It won't do, to offer a book worth the money, and receive your dollar with the air of a beggar soliciting alms !

It won't do, to walk Broadway an hour before you can muster courage to offer your book at all ! *I know.*

It won't do, to feel put down because

you chance to be the nineteenth, who has offered to sell, in that very place, that very day, before dinner!

No. Boldly approach, and assume to confer a favor.

Come straight from your home to your customer.

Bless you! it is the nineteenth woman who makes the trade.

What matter, if they can buy to better advantage elsewhere? make them buy of *you*.

I am not "strong minded;" but I pity the men of nowadays. Alongside the women, their chance is slim!

"Bloody Mary" is said to have re-marked, "that in death, 'Calais' would be found printed upon her heart!"

Not "Calais," but "Mexico," is imprinted in letters of fire upon my heart, and head too!

Every nerve, of an exhausted vitality, responds to the assertion that she is indeed, our " Sister Republic."

Had I roamed the " Halls of the Montezumas " republican at heart ; and — immortal as the " Wandering Jew " — walked down the Years, to that freed land of to-day; I could not more persistently have laid before New York and Boston, this ephemeral fact.

Facing wind and weather ; bearing

"A Banner with this strange device,"

I passed on.

I went into " Wall " Street with awe ; into "Broad " Street with hope.

Had not the fascination of the female element, thrown its charm and romance over the " bread and butter business " of " stock brokerage ? "

I drew near. —

Directly before me, in large letters upon the door, was this notice :

" BEGGARS AND PEDDLERS NOT ADMITTED."

Meekly I slipped in ; passed a long row of industrious clerks; and entered — the " Sanctum."

The " Presidential Candidate " was flitting about, gracefully button-holing a very good looking — I wonder who it could be ? — brother financier.

The soliciting partner, at lady-like ease, was softly humming,

> "Will you walk into my parlor ?
>   Said the spider to the fly."

Seizing a favorable opportunity, I spoke to them of my errand.

" Madame! responded the ' Candidate,' if ' General Grant' and the ' Angel Gabriel indorsed your book, WE should not invest in ' Mexico ! ''

Subsiding into my normal condition of " a worm of the dust," I crawled away.

But I came from the " Grand Opera House," proud to show upon my subscription page the name of New York's, public-spirited, magnificent, "*un bon vivant.*"

I came from "Bunker Hill," glorying in names whose fathers fought, bled, and died, for Liberty!

Not having "nine children and one at the breast," I was thrown upon the bare merits of the work; and I am free to say, those merits have never failed me.

I have had the pleasure and the honor, of introducing Colonel Albert S. Evans' reliable, and very readable, production into many of our first families.

Excuse my laughing! It is at this recollection.

In Boston there dwells a bachelor; very rich, and — I will be charitable — very close.

Still, he had known me "egg and bird," and I was sure of my man.

Confidently presenting to him my " Mex ican " claim, he patronizingly patted me on the shoulder, his face all of a yard long, and informed me, in sepulchral tones, that he had just lost fifty thousand dollars; that he would be happy to buy some other day!

" Mexico " was at a discount; her budding hopes crushed out of sight by the magnitude of this loss, which I considerately gave him four months to recover.

The breezy, exhilarating zephyrs of March wafted me again in that direction.

His face drawn to precisely the same angle; his shoulder pats precisely as sympathetic; his voice precisely as hollow; he said he was now arranging his business, and urged me to come by and by!

Reckoning by years, it is time that man's affairs were settled.

Reckoning by money, it is time that man was bled to the tune of one subscription book, at least.

Imitating the euphonious harmony of the primer rhyme

> " Zaccheus he
> Did climb a tree " —

I announce to thee, bachelor mine —

> "I shall call
> In the fall."

But as to the Biblical student there would be keen, though perhaps obscure, satire, in the transposition of the lines;

> "In the *Fall*
> I shall call."

How this avocation sharpens the wits!

As to the human countenance, it becomes so transparent that an "agent" must be stupid indeed who cannot read as he runs.

What variety too, in manner!

Some, kind and generous; others, polite and mean; some, indifferent and morose; and others, downright rude, with curses not "loud but deep," speed you on your way.

Seeking the first; shunning the last; I have been brought mostly into contact with the agreeable.

My Mexico's fair list, boasts names " men delight to honor;" as well as those of personal friends to the distinguished party, who made the "Gala Trip" through her gorgeous Tropics!

Fellow-laborer, in this inviting field, look to thyself! "Be ye wise as a serpent, harmless as a dove."

Fellow-laborer, gird thyself! Names of note have preceded thee. May not Paul, Apostle to the Gentiles, in his earlier years, have been engaged in this business?

Does not his assertion, that he was all things to all men, hoping thereby to gain *some*, smack of an experience evolved as an "Agent?" At all events, the whole secret of success is inclosed in this very nutshell, "all things to all men." In these days, the chances are *you* will thereby gain the lot.

I know one — young and handsome; who, by close observance of this rule, made his "pile" out of a last year's almanac; better still; out of a pamphlet far more un-

interesting and *passè* than any modern almanac; for, under the able generalship of a
well-known humorist, " Allmanax " are taking a lead in literature!

I know another — of education and address; who failed to earn his salt, though
showing a work indorsed by the first in the
land, through lack of the " Chameleon " in
his nature.

But I know a woman — long may she
wave! — who, to unprecedented tact in
swelling a subscription list, unites consum-
mate shrewdness in making herself good
against possible loss; thus eminently com-
bining the two essential points, of " raising
the wind," and when " raised," of appropri-
ating the same: the capacity to do which,
in a more enlarged sphere, would place her
'bull," or " bear," in the front rank, as a
Wall Street financier!

I declare; was I myself to start a subscription book, and that person applied to

15

me for a chance, such is my admiration of her as a "success," that notwithstanding a certain looseness respecting "meum et tuum," I would appoint her canvasser in-chief over any district she might desire. "*Sauve qui peut.*"

CHAPTER XXXV.

THE " HUB."

" There always shall be one to bless ; for I am on thy side."

In New York I was comparatively a stranger; but they "did not take me in," either figuratively or literally.

Only the Omnipotent can reckon the prayers that silently go up, on "the wings of the morning," from the streets of that gay metropolis for help; for material aid; which can that day, only be realized by Heaven itself!

My last book was sold.

At the end of five months, I too, fell into the ranks of the great multitude who throng her streets with burdened hearts; and — nothing to do.

Per necessity I returned to Boston; in-debted a second time, to the kindness of a friend, for a " free pass."

There I was well known; and sure at least of one acquaintance within her classic limits, who would not suffer me to starve.

I was now, sole and undisputed owner of a purple and black, striped gown (how glad I am I was persuaded six years ago at Jordan & Marsh's into buying it; a firmer piece of goods was never thrown upon Boston Market).

I was now, sole and undisputed owner of a " water-proof " (more ancient, equally abid-ing).

And — my reputation !

Financially, this was bad. But morally — here I made a stand.

When I leave the Metropolitan city; come on " *via* " Springfield; and get out at the Boston and Albany depot; the order and cleanliness before me, is in grateful contrast to the confusion and filth I have left behind.

Quietness reigns. The sky is blue. The air pure; and bracing — with the thermometer at zero, and a stiff gale from the Northwest!

I set my feet upon historic soil.

Abode too of the fine ·arts; nowhere beside so critically appreciated.

Mecca of genius! Centre of triumphs! climaxed by the " Peace Jubilee."

Athenians of America! justly art thou proud of thine Athens, creation's Hub!

Are my proclivities downward? Am I of the "earth, earthy?" Do I fraternize with *dirt?*

If, after this, I own right up, and say, " Give me New York for better or for worse;" all Boston will howl back in the affirmative.

But listen —

Once more at home, where the greater part of my life had been spent, my heart swelled with gratitude that I was again one of thy citizens; O, Puritanical city of Boston!

To be sure, within thy walls I had waded through seas of sorrow; but, let the "Past bury its own dead."

I hoped to commence life anew.

I have a cousin who, in the course of his half century life, has brought forth two original remarks.

One, I have already given; the other, declared poverty to be an unmitigated curse!

I protested. In the first place, the dear companionship of friends would alleviate the evil; in the second place, education would rob it of its sting; in the third place, one's own consciousness of talent and mother wit, would come to the rescue;

in the fourth place, the world owed everybody a living; which everybody was a fool
if he did not get.

The reticence of my cousin was his chief
virtue. *That* was good for the brief re-
sponse, " TRY IT ! "

Years have elapsed. I *have* tried it; and
am prepared to say — the wisdom of the
godlike Socrates; the sage Plato; the practical Confucius — *pale* before the transcend-
ent utterance of that man !

Not to discuss the question of what the
world really owes; it is stereotyped, that it
is a mighty hard thing now-a-days to make
her pay her just debts.

Talent, I hold to be terribly in the way,
unless it has a wider field than poverty can
afford, in which to follow its bent, and —
operate.

What you are pleased to consider your
" mother wit," be very careful not to venti-
late, unless you are tolerably situated in a
worldly point of view.

You can neither say, nor do, a smart thing in reduced circumstances.

How dare you expect your talent, or your wit to be appreciated, if you have lost your money? " *Qui perde pèche.*"

Poor unfortunate ! " be not deceived ; " the people " are not mocked ; " whatever your own conception of ability, others will not recognize it, unless set in gold !

As to education to while the hours of poverty —— well ! this is a delicate question ; but, at the risk of offending the scholastic, I reiterate ; that the most important branch of knowledge, next " Our Lord's Prayer," to be instilled — at least into the youthful, female mind — is the complex art of modern cookery !

Then, a certain livelihood is secured ; no thanks to " Belles-lettres " or mathematics !

CHAPTER XXXVI.

THE RECEPTION.

"Going with gayly in the morning to woo the world with smiles."

"Is met by those way-faring men with coldness, suspicion, and repulse."

But the dear companionship of friends? — *there* I have you!

"Thou fool!" dost thou not know, that — in poverty — thy friendships are a myth!

Take a walk down Washington Street any fine day, and learn for yourself.

Before you reach the "Old South" the fact will be patent.

It was patented to *me* on this wise —

Entering a leading store in that fashion-able locality, I was received as a stranger

No. Strangers are entitled to courtesy. I was met, as would be the foul scum of society, for daring to float in that debarred direction; and yet, in the by-gone days, many is the time I have tripped on "light fantastic toe" to the merry music of "Fisher's Hornpipe," with the very person who thus ignored me!

Amid all my humiliations it was the first time, but by no means the last, that I had been so strangely regarded; and as the final "feather to the camel's back," *that* completely broke me down. I passed the remainder of the day in tears.

I would not shed so many again, though all my quondam acquaintance should rise "*en masse*," to crush me back into my original elements. Not much!

And another — in whose veins every drop of blood flowing, is as mine — but let him pass! I fancy upon the occasion of that well improved opportunity, he who readeth can understand, with the heart searching-glare of my wrathful eyes, I managed to avenge myself — and scorch him!

And another — who, in the far-off hours of girlish intimacy, had so entwined herself around my heart-strings, that every memory of those happiest times but flash before me her laughing face, looked coldly; nay worse; believed me capable of winking at ˙ deeds, the abhorred conception of which caused my very soul to shudder!

My reputation! the conviction was forced upon me; an enemy had surely tampered with that. I know —

"A look may work thy ruin, or a word create thy wealth"—

but could so foul a slander have arisen from this?

While absent, I kept house four weeks. During that time two disreputable individuals contrived to insinuate themselves into my good graces; and through ignorance of their style, become inmates of the family.

Ascertaining the truth, they had but short notice to leave.

The odium of this affair, trifling as it was, so thoroughly disturbed me; that I immediately sacrificed every advantage, and gave up my new home.

In my great need; and though perse-cuted, as it were, for very righteousness' sake; many believed in good faith that, in the city of New York, I was the prosperous mistress of a — house of ILL FAME!

Believed; that the innocent girl; the close student; the happy wife; the desolate widow; the wretched victim of another's in-temperance; could be so lost to herself, to her friends; to her God; as to countenance a life, the "steps to which take hold on hell!"

But one, raised his voice in my behalf.

But one, contradicted the vile aspersion.

On my bended knees have I returned thanks to the All Powerful for raising me up the "one" friend, in that, my direst need.

No longer do I wonder, that despairing kinsfolk so often seek to recognize their dead at the gloomy *Morgue !*

And the other; would I could give his name! who, in mercy, saved *me* from that last, sad resting-place.

With words of sympathy; offers of aid; he brought me back to hope; and his persistent, Christian kindness —

Held me back — from appearing unsummoned, before the " Unknown!"

Held me back — from the unblest future of the deliberate "Suicide!"

CHAPTER XXXVII.

"OUR LORD'S PRAYER."

"Our Father who art in heaven,
    Hallowed be thy name.
    Thy kingdom come.
Thy will be done on earth as it is in heaven.
    Give us this day our daily bread.
And forgive us our trespasses, as we forgive those who trespass
    against us.
And lead us not into temptation, but deliver us from evil;
For thine is the kingdom, and the power,
And the glory — forever — Amen."

    "Now I lay me down to sleep;
    I pray the Lord my soul to keep.
    If I should die before I wake—
    I pray the Lord my soul to take."

IT IS PAST!

Day is softly fading in the west. Night is gently coming to the earth.

I sit in my quiet room; and Memory

forgetful of my blessings; faithful to but half her mission; spreads out before me the loss of my youth, my ambition, my property, my reputation!

Serenely I consider this absence of all the world calls good.

From the bitter ashes of earthly disappointment has arisen upon my vision, the heavenly Star of Hope!

I lift mine eyes —

They fall upon my youthful husband; the man to whom, before angels and men, I have sworn to be true.

"Clothed, and in his right mind," he is sitting by my side.

He is making an honest effort to reform.

He is engaged in useful labor.

Curses, are exchanged for prayers; blows, for loving words; prodigality, for Christian economy.

And — as he falls upon his knees before me — humbly, and with tears, imploring my forgiveness for the great wrong he has done; the words, " *Forgive us our trespasses, as we forgive those who trespass against us;* " burn in letters of fire upon the wall; and I KNOW it would be at the peril of my soul, to refuse.

He, forgiven, will cover a multitude of my sins!

Here, I have had tribulation!

Hereafter, face to face with the ABSOLUTE, I shall have compensation!

" At even time it will be light."

THE END.

www.ingramcontent.com/pod-product-compliance
Lightning Source LLC
Chambersburg PA
CBHW022006050726
47499CB00006BB/1755